BUDDIES, BULLIES, AND BASEBALL

Buddies, Bullies, and Baseball

PHYLLIS J. PERRY

ISBN: 978-1-63161-051-6

Published by TCK Publishing

www.TCKPublishing.com

Get discounts and special deals on our best-selling books at

www.TCKPublishing.com/bookdeals

DEDICATION

For Katherine

CONTENTS

CHAPTER 1

I squeezed my eyes together as tight as I could, praying that when I opened them again, the two distant figures that I saw leaning against the fence wouldn't be there. But I knew better. The sick feeling in the pit of my stomach was proof enough that they were real. When I opened my eyes and screwed up the courage to look again. I confirmed what I already knew: straight ahead of me, waiting, were Steve Mates and his buddy, Cliff. And I knew they were waiting for me.

It had started late last May, just before school let out. This fall, I thought maybe they'd forgotten about me. They hadn't. Seeing them here this morning meant that they were starting it all up again, three weeks into the new school year. They would take what they wanted whenever they wanted, and humiliate me while I did nothing. I felt sick.

"Hey, Mustard," Steve said as soon as I stepped through the opening in the fence onto the playground. He strode up and poked me in the shoulder as he spoke. Not a friendly poke, but one that really hurt, though not as much as hearing again the name Steve had given me last May. He'd taunted me then, saying that I had a real yellow streak. And he was right. I was a coward.

"Hey," I mumbled in reply, as I tried to walk on by. Dumb move. I knew they weren't going to let me go.

"What's your hurry?" Cliff demanded, reaching out to grab me by the backpack and bringing me to a halt. I balled my hands into fists, but didn't raise my arms.

Cliff roughly unzipped my pack as I stood there feeling helpless. He pulled out the lunch sack which was on top and tossed it to Steve. Taking his time as if he enjoyed every second of it, Steve reached inside the sack. He pulled out the bag containing my sandwich and wrinkled up his nose.

"Ugh! Tuna." He sniffed the air in disgust and dropped the sandwich back inside. Next he pulled out an apple, made a little grunt of disapproval, and threw it over his shoulder onto the grass. "But not a total loss," he added as he pulled out the package of twin chocolate cupcakes.

Taking these, he dropped my lunch sack in the dirt and ambled off. "Later," he said over his shoulder as he left followed by a grinning Cliff. I watched as Steve tore open the pack, threw the wrapper on the ground, and handed one cupcake to Cliff, while he took a big chomp out of the other. I hoped he'd choke on it.

I walked over and picked up my apple, rubbed it clean against my jeans, and dropped it back into the lunch sack. I reached around and put the bag back in my pack. I kept my head down, hoping no one was watching out here at the far end of the playground.

I trudged toward the school building, passing the climbing structure that the first graders played on. It was rough timber in the shape of a fort, with lots of ladders and rings. A little guy in a yellow and navy striped shirt stepped off the top of one of the ladders and made a grab for the big ring. The ring slipped out of his hands and he fell with a plop. I think he had the wind knocked out of him because for a second or two, he said and did nothing but look surprised. Then a wail went up.

I hesitated, glancing toward two parents who were talking away, leaning against the corner of the building. Clearly they didn't notice. The kid reminded me a little of myself in first grade: scrawny, with red hair that fell in his eyes. I didn't think the little guy was really hurt, but I couldn't walk off and leave him. So I went over.

"Hi, there, buddy," I said.

He looked at me wide-eyed, as if wondering who the heck I was. I stood him up and dusted him off a bit. "You know, I used to have trouble with that ring, too," I said. "Go on back up the ladder and I'll help."

He looked at me for a minute and hesitated. Then he climbed back up the ladder and eyed the ring.

I grabbed the ring and pushed it over to him. He reached out, got both hands around it and swung off. Triumphantly, he hung there for a minute before dropping to the ground, landing on his feet this time. "Thanks," he said before running off to the slide.

I continued on toward the wing that held my fifth-grade classroom. The bell rang before I got there, so I joined the back of the line and filed on in. After dropping my backpack in the coat closet, I took my seat, leaning over to talk to my best friends, C.J. and Lizabeth, who sat at the same work table with me. They looked enough alike to be brother and sister—both short, with dark hair and eyes. I avoided looking across the room at Steve, who I knew would be smirking at me.

After a few minutes, I sat down and turned part way around; the fourth seat at our table, usually left vacant, was filled this morning. Sitting in the chair right next to me was a large kid with a lot of curly blonde hair. He smiled, but I was still conscious of Steve staring at me and I was in no mood to be friendly, so I ignored him. Lots of the other kids were looking over our way, too.

After the second bell rang, Mrs. Hollis quickly took role and hot lunch count, jotted the tallies on a slip of paper, and put it in the pocket on the hallway door. Then she turned to face the class.

"Good morning," she said with a big smile, and walked over to our table. "I want you to meet a new student." She stood behind the new kid's chair. "This is Hans Ollig. He's moved here from Germany, where he lived in the town of Landstiehl." As she spoke, she walked over to the wall, pulled down a map, and pointed out a town. "It's just a couple miles from Ramstein Air Base where his stepfather was a transport pilot in the United States Air Force. Welcome, Hans."

"Is he here for a visit, or is he going to stay?" a student asked.

"He's going to stay," Mrs. Hollis replied. "Boulder is his new home. Please make him feel welcome. Jack, I'll ask you to be his special buddy today and show him around."

She smiled down at me as if she'd handed me a present. I felt myself giving her a dopey smile in return because I couldn't think of anything to say. I mean, how do you blurt out, "Thanks, but no thanks. I've got enough problems?"

Every now and then, I said something to the new kid, like, "Do you need a pencil?" He'd smile, friendly enough, but never spoke a word.

At morning recess, C.J. and I took Hans with us and showed him the boys' bathroom. Lizabeth joined us out on the playground. I had been keeping my eye out for Steve, looking over my shoulder. It wasn't easy to miss him. He had short, spiky hair, and was one of the biggest kids in fifth grade. Not fat. Just big. I saw him way up on the baseball field where my buddies and I usually went. Today I led the way over to one of the basketball courts where we joined some kids in shooting baskets.

C. J. and Lizabeth didn't act too surprised at my heading for the basketball court. I guess they thought I was doing something different in honor of Hans. We watched for a minute or two, so that Hans could see how it went. Someone threw you the ball, and you took a shot. Then you ran up underneath the basket to retrieve the ball and toss it to the next person before you ran back and joined the line again. Not much to it. Hans made a few and missed a few baskets, nothing special, but he seemed to be having fun.

"Do you speak any English?" Lizabeth asked Hans as she stood behind him.

Leave it to Liz, I thought, to come right out and ask a dumb question. Didn't she hear that this kid was German?

Hans hesitantly replied, *"Ein bischen* — a little."

My jaw must have fallen open. That was news to me. Those were the first words he'd spoken all morning.

"What street do you live on?" Lizabeth asked, and she talked perfectly normal, not slow or loud or anything, even if he was German.

"Emerson *Strasse,* Street," Hans answered.

Another surprise. That was just a few blocks away from where C.J., Liz, and I all lived.

When the recess bell rang, Lizabeth grabbed Hans' arm and said, "C'mon. Let's step on it." She turned and started jogging toward our classroom door.

Hans jogged along beside her. *"Step on it?"* I heard him say, looking puzzled.

Lizabeth laughed. "That just means we've got to hurry up so we aren't late."

"Ah," Hans said, and I almost heard the 'click' as he added that to his memory bank of English words.

During the math lesson that morning, Mrs. Hollis reviewed multiplication of fractions. She wrote a couple of problems on the white erase board, showing how to convert to the lowest denominator. Then she assigned a few problems from our math book and walked around the class, checking to see how everyone was doing.

Math was my favorite period of the day. It came easy to me. C.J. was good at math too, and Lizabeth was a whiz at almost everything. Hans watched to see what book we were using, and he pulled his out and set right to work. He seemed to know what he was doing.

When Ms. Hollis got to our table she said, "Hey! Good for you. Perfect scores all around." I guess German numbers must be the same as American numbers.

Reading came next, and it was an independent reading day. Everyone had a book to read and some sheets to fill out when it was completed. The sheets had a bunch of questions like who was the author, title, and main characters. It was a pain to fill out the sheets, but I liked independent reading day. You actually had time to read while Mrs. Hollis held what she called "conferences" one-on-one with students. The book I was reading, *Stealing Home,* was a really good baseball story.

Mrs. Hollis called Hans up to her desk. I glanced over and saw that Lizabeth was already deep into her latest fantasy-mystery book, something called *The Maifix.* As usual, C.J.'s seat was already empty. He always tried to make himself invisible on independent reading days as he slipped out to go to another classroom to work with a few other kids and the Chapter I reading teacher. I didn't talk about it much with C.J. because I knew it embarrassed him to be getting special reading help, so I never understood what "Chapter I" was. But I didn't think you ever got to Chapter II, because C. J. had been in Chapter I for three years now.

I had only read a sentence or two when I heard a crash at the back of the room. Everyone looked up to stare. On his way to the door, C.J. had stumbled, or so it looked. Since this happened right by Steve's desk, it was likely that Steve had stuck out his foot and tripped C.J. I was pretty sure Steve picked on him, too, but that was another thing C.J. and I never talked about. At the moment, Steve was the only one not staring at C.J. He was innocently reading his book as if he were totally caught up in some wonderful story. C.J. didn't say anything. He just left the room.

After Ms. Hollis had spent a few minutes with Hans, he came back to the table with a book in hand. I glanced over, curious to see if he was reading a book that had English words in it. He was, and it wasn't a baby picture book, but a pretty fat book called *The Sky Phantom,* so I guessed maybe he could read English better than he could speak it..

C.J. slipped back into our classroom just before lunch. I'd been waiting for him to come back. I noticed he took a roundabout way from the door to reach our table. My guess was he was avoiding going anywhere near Steve Mates.

"Time to get your things for lunch," Mrs. Hollis announced.

During the general hubbub of people putting away books and going to the closet to get lunches and jackets, I managed a few words with him.

"You made a lot of noise when you left this morning," I said. "Was that thanks to Steve Mates, or were you just stumbling over your big feet?"

He frowned but only said, "My feet aren't that big."

He didn't say anything else, but I knew exactly how he felt. Mad and helpless. I mean, what could you do? If you actually complained to the teacher, everyone would think you were a tattletale. And somehow Steve never got caught in the act. He was a genius at pulling these stunts of his when no adult could see him.

As we grabbed our lunch sacks and headed out the door and down the hall toward the lunch room, I grudgingly said to Hans, "Come on. It's time for chow."

"Chow?" Hans repeated after me, puzzled.

"Time for lunch," Lizabeth explained as she stepped up behind us.

"Ah," Hans said, understanding. "*Chow.* Lunch. Let's step on it."

Lizabeth and C.J. laughed, and even I managed a little grin. Give credit where it's due. This guy was trying.

As soon as we entered the cafeteria, we were hit by a wave of noise.. No one was actually shouting or misbehaving, but that many kids in that little space made a lot of racket. And our noses was assaulted, too. Very spicy. Tacos today?

C.J. was buying a hot lunch, so he split off to get a tray. I bought a box of milk, and then headed off with Lizabeth and Hans in tow for an empty table. We found one that had been wiped clean, and we grabbed it. As soon as he'd gone through the line, C.J. picked up his tray and joined us. I tried not to look too longingly at the brownies in Lizabeth's lunch, or the three chocolate-chip cookies that Hans had spread out on a napkin in front of him. Even the chocolate pudding from the school lunch looked pretty good to me. All I had was a tuna fish sandwich and a bruised apple. I tried not to think about it.

Then Steve and Cliff crowded in at the table across from us. Speaking just loudly enough to be heard by all of us, but well under the general din and the hearing of the lunch room monitor, Steve started his needling..

"Too bad we're not having hot dogs today," he said, "since we have Mustard right here at our table."

Cliff laughed loudly as if this were the funniest thing he'd ever heard.

"And who's Mustard slumming around with today? Why, it looks like a Nazi and a retardo."

Again Steve's sidekick laughed.

At the mention of the word "Nazi," Hans looked up from his lunch and frowned. He glanced first at Steve and then at me. "Was ist?" he said, and then immediately corrected himself. "Who is he calling Nazi? What is 'retardo?'"

I felt my face heating up with embarrassment. This is what I'd worried about this morning when Mrs. Hollis assigned me as a buddy to Hans. It was bad news for both of us. The insults were partially lost on Hans, but clearly he had enough smarts to know that something ugly was being said.

I glanced over at C.J. He was continuing to eat his taco but at this point, he seemed to be having trouble swallowing. I glared at Steve but said nothing.

Meantime, Hans still looked as if he was waiting for some sort of an explanation.

Steve couldn't leave it alone. "Awfully quiet across the table, isn't it, Cliff? Except maybe for the Red Baron, or whoever he is. I think he's mumbling something, but I can't quite make it out."

More laughter from Cliff.

"Cut it out," Lizabeth said, and she stared straight at Steve.

"Oooh, oooh," Steve squealed. "I do believe Little Miss Perfect has something to say."

"Yeah, in fact, I do," Lizabeth said, softly but firmly. "Leave us alone, or you're going to be sorry."

"Ooh. I'm so scared. Me, afraid of Miss Perfect, a Nazi, a Retardo, and Mustard?" Steve snorted. "Not likely."

I watched, unable to say or do anything, as Lizabeth stood. Slowly and carefully, she picked up the cup in front of her that she had filled with orange juice from her Thermos. In no hurry, she walked around the end of the table to where Steve sat. Then she poured the whole cup of juice onto his shoulder and down his lap.

"Yikes!" Steve yelled, partially jumping up.

"Oh, dear," Lizabeth shouted, loudly enough to catch the cafeteria monitor's attention. "Did I spill something on you? Oh, dear."

What an actress. Lizabeth's face was the picture of dismay.

The cafeteria monitor came hurrying over with a damp cloth and a handful of paper towels. Lizabeth, with an innocent look on her face, helped clean up the few drops that had actually made it to the floor, while the manager mopped at the table, where there was also surprisingly little to clean up. The vast majority of juice had somehow landed on and soaked into Steve's shirt and pants. Furious, but unable to say anything, he dabbed helplessly at himself with paper towels.

Lizabeth snatched up another paper towel and dabbed roughly at Steve's head, as in a perfectly serious voice she said to the cafeteria manger, "That juice went everywhere!"

I'm not sure if anyone else but Lizabeth could have pulled that off. C.J. was grinning from ear to ear, and so was Hans. He might not have known all the details of what had just happened, but he definitely got most of it.

Lizabeth then serenely returned to her place at the table, turned to Hans, and said, "Now, what was it we were talking about?"

As soon as the cafeteria monitor left, Steve glared, not at Lizabeth but right at me, as he said, "You're lucky to have a girl stand up for you today, loser, but you can't hide behind her for long." He climbed to his feet. "See ya tomorrow."

CHAPTER 2

Dad and I sat glued in front of the TV set in the family room, while my mom went back and forth to and from the kitchen. I don't really understand her. She likes baseball all right, but not the way my dad and I do. I mean, she can walk out of the room when the count is three and two. I've seen her do it. But that's good, because it means she heats and serves pizza and refills the popcorn bowl for us. Of course, Dad and I do all the cleanup, but only after the last batter's out.

During big games like this one, the three of us sit on the couch, me in the middle, with the popcorn bowl in my lap. We were already on our second bowl tonight. It was the bottom of the eighth inning, and the Rockies were hanging on to a one-run lead.

Any night involving our beloved Colorado Rockies would have been a lot like this. But this wasn't just any game. This was the National League Championship Series, and it had gone all the way, three games apiece for the Colorado Rockies and the Philadelphia Phillies. Tonight was it, an on-the-road, now-or-never, do-or-die game. If the Rockies won, our team would be in the World Series for only the second time ever. And if we lost, I didn't want to even think about it. Right now, the Phillies had two runners on base and two out.

"Yes!" Dad yelled. "Yes!" as he jumped to his feet and pumped a fist into the air. A long fly ball to center field had retired the side, and the Phillies were trudging back to their dugout.

I jumped up, too, first handing off the bowl of popcorn to Mom. Dad and I exchanged high fives and did a little dance of joy before plopping down again only to scrunch forward on the edge of our seats.

"Now, what we need is a little insurance," Dad said, clapping his hands, as he leaned forward. "A little hustle, hustle. An extra run or two wouldn't hurt a bit."

Dad often yelled encouragement to the team members as if they could hear him through the TV set. Who knows? Maybe it made a difference. I know it did for me in the summer during our ball games when I could hear his voice above all the others, yelling in the dugout for me or one of my teammates. He was our assistant baseball coach. I heard someone ask him once if he was the batting coach or the pitching coach.

He said, "Neither. I'm the cheerleader."

And he really was. I knew I was lucky that he spent time with me and the team. Of course, some of the other parents attended most of our games, too, but others never came even once, and some were just plain poor sports. If we lost, there was a lot of venting, more from the adults than the kids. Never from Dad. Oh, Dad liked winning. We all did. But I never saw him get down in the dumps no matter what the score. He always looked proud of the way I played, win or lose.

I remember one night last July when we'd lost a game seventeen to one. Talk about a disgrace. Dad still took all of us out afterwards to the ice cream shop for sundaes, and within five minutes he had us all laughing and having a good time, too.

Steve Mates played on a different summer baseball team, the same one that Cliff was on. I knew for a fact that Steve hated his team captain, Billy Batasso. Steve had wanted to be captain himself. We were playing them a game one night, and Billy dropped a fly ball. Cliff gave Billy a hard time, and kept teasing him about it. That's when Steve claimed Cliff for his best buddy. From that time on, Steve and Cliff were inseparable.

Suddenly, in the midst of the night's happiness and excitement, I frowned. Remembering that awful game last July made me think of Steve Mates. He had a reputation as a home run hitter. He'd been at the ice cream shop that night, too, across the room from us. Steve had been on the winning team. During a burst of laughter from our table, I remembered him glaring at me as if I had no right to celebrate losing.

I didn't want Dad to know I was a coward. I was afraid he'd be so disappointed in me if he found out that I was letting Steve bully me, and that I didn't even try to stand up for myself. And nothing could be worse than disappointing my dad.

Quickly I brushed those ugly thoughts aside. There was no time for them now.

This was the last inning of the game. The first Rockies batter was up. A sharp little hit into short left field was enough. Base hit. A long fly ball caught deep in left field advanced the runner to second base. My heart climbed into my throat as the next batter struck out.

At this point, Mom went out to the kitchen and poured another cup of coffee. Can you believe it? Calm as you please, she just walked out. My dog, Echo, a little black-and-white mutt with one ear that stood up and another that flopped down, followed after her, ever-hopeful for a tidbit of some kind. By the time she got back, the new batter had a full count, three and two. I was holding my breath even though I kept telling myself, "Hey! We're still ahead by one run. Breathe."

Then came the most beautiful sound you'll ever hear: the crack of the bat. That ball was hit deep, deep into left field. The batter watched the ball as he headed down the first baseline. The fielder went back, back, and jumped as high as he could against the wall. Home run! The hitter made a ceremonial run around the bases before being mobbed at home plate.

Dad and I did another little dance. A three-run lead. We had the insurance runs my dad had hoped for. In my joy, I tossed a piece of popcorn to Echo, who caught it neatly. No matter that the next Rocky batter fouled out to the catcher. We headed into the bottom of the ninth, and our pitcher hung on, retiring three batters in succession. It was over! The Colorado Rockies were going to the World Series.

Pure joy erupted on the field and in our living room, too. Euphoria carried me through the process of cleaning up, brushing my teeth, and getting ready for bed. Then I lay there with eyes wide open. Sleep wouldn't come. My Rockies were headed to the World Series.

CHAPTER 3

I must have finally dozed off though, because suddenly my alarm clock was ringing. The first thought on waking up was about the World Series. Then came the second thought. School. This brought with it a sickening worry about Steve Mates. What could I do? Would he be there, waiting? Would I be a push-over again?

As I munched on my breakfast cereal and cinnamon toast, I made a plan. I'd take a little detour from my usual walk to school. Actually, this route wasn't a little detour, it was a lot farther, but it brought me in on the opposite side of the back playground field.

When I arrived, no one was waiting by that gate. With a sigh of relief, I started walking toward the school building. I hadn't come far when I heard a voice behind me.

"Hey, there, Mustard!"

I whirled around, and there was Steve.

"Were you exploring new ways to school today? No need, you know, because all roads lead to me." Somehow he and Cliff had spotted me from across the playground and managed to quickly circle around and come up behind me.

"Just hold your horses," Cliff said, grabbing me by my backpack and holding me in one spot. He unzipped my pack and pulled out my lunch sack, tossing it to Steve.

"Where are your Nazi and Retardo buddies this morning?" Steve asked, pretending to look for them. "And little Miss Perfect, your bodyguard." Cliff snickered at that last comment.

Steve pulled out my sandwich. "PB&J," he said, rejecting it and dropping it back into the sack. "But, hey, hey, hey! What have we here?" He pulled out a small bag of chips and a plastic baggie containing two of my Mom's chocolate-iced brownies. He held them both high in one hand. "Not bad." There was also a bright orange clementine, and Steve grabbed and tossed it as far as he could across the field.

Dropping my lunch sack onto the dirt, Steve said, "Later, Mustard," and ambled off toward the school building with Cliff walking beside him. I couldn't catch what they said, but there was more laughter as they tossed away the plastic baggie and turned to stare back at me. I watched them wolfing down my brownies.

I stared out toward my clementine. I'd probably be hungry at lunch, but I'd look like a dog playing fetch if I went hunting for it now. I felt so bad, I just wanted to go home and curl up in bed. But how could I explain that? Pretend to be sick? Tell Mom and Dad that I was a yellow coward unable to stand up for myself? What was wrong with me anyway? Why didn't I throw a punch and just get beat up? I know that Mom always said, "No problem is ever solved with fists," but there was a lot she didn't understand. Finally, not knowing what else to do, I picked up my almost-empty lunch sack and trudged down toward the fifth grade wing. The first bell rang just before I got in line.

I mumbled a 'hey' to the three at my table, but pretended to be very involved in writing something in my notebook. I was just making meaningless doodles, but it gave me an excuse not to talk to anyone.

"What's wrong?" C.J. whispered. "I thought you'd be on Cloud Nine. Wasn't that a great game last night?"

"Yeah," I agreed, and I felt a little grin turning up the edges of my mouth. "How about them Rockies!"

But the happy glow didn't last long. It seemed whenever I looked across the room, I could see Steve smirking at me. Mrs. Hollis started the math lesson, but I couldn't get into it. I felt like some sort of bug being examined under Steve's microscope. Normally, I didn't have any math difficulties. Numbers were pretty straightforward, and I think anybody in our room would have listed me as one of the best math students in the class.

But my math superiority didn't extend to dividing fractions. I could do the problems, but I didn't really "get it." The steps were simple enough: you just took the fraction you wanted to divide by, turned it upside down and called it the reciprocal. I didn't know why, and I didn't care. Next, you multiplied the top numbers of the first fraction and the top of the reciprocal and multiplied the *bottom* numbers of the first fraction by the *bottom* number of the reciprocal, and you got a new number. But why? You got me! Every time I tried to figure it out, my eyes started crossing.

Dividing fractions was just plain weird. Most of the time in math, I could find simple reasons for how you might use something in real life that you learned in math. I mean, if there were thirty kids in the room, and you wanted to divide them into four baseball teams, how many kids would be on each team? I could see why you needed to divide by four, and I understood that remainders meant that some teams would have one more than others. But why would anyone ever want to divide one-half by one-fourth? Seriously.

Mrs. Hollis had been droning on for quite some time now about division being the inverse of multiplying, and frankly I wasn't listening. I was thinking of some way to get through the lunch hour without being humiliated by Steve, and replaying over and over Steve making off with my chips and brownies.

The room was quiet. Mrs. Hollis had stopped talking. Suddenly I was aware that not just Steve, but everyone in the room was staring at me, and that my name hung in the air. Mrs. Hollis must have called on me while my thoughts were miles away, and I hadn't the faintest idea what the question was, let alone the answer. I shot a quick look around the table. Hans was smiling, C.J. and Lizabeth seemed to be confidently waiting for me to say something brilliant. Panicked, I looked up at the white erase board.

Chances were that the problem up there was what I was being asked about. Sure enough, there was a division of fractions problem, neatly laid out: 6/8 divided by 3/8 equals? Quickly, I inverted, and multiplied, but I was still thinking about the morning incident, and somehow I blurted out, "Two brownies."

For a moment there was silence, and then a roar of laughter, coming loudest of course from Steve's corner of the room. I couldn't believe I'd said that. I felt my face burning.

Mrs. Hollis smiled and said, "Jack, you're absolutely right. The answer is two."

Without missing a beat, she went on with something about if you had a whole number like 75 and divided it by a faction like 3/4, it was like multiplying 75 by 4 and dividing it by 3 which gives you 100, or something like that which made absolutely no sense. But at least it got the kids all looking back at her instead of at me.

Somehow I made it through the rest of the morning. At recess, I suffered a few brownie jokes from my classmates, but fortunately everyone just thought I was hungry and teased me about my appetite. Only Steve and Cliff knew better, and I made it a point to keep as far away from them as I could.

Finally, it was lunch time, and I picked up my pitifully light lunch sack and the baseball cap and ball I'd brought with me to school. I pushed on up to the line at the door, making no effort whatsoever to connect with Hans. Lizabeth and C.J. were right behind me and C.J. was carrying a bat.

"Hey!" Lizabeth said. "What about Hans?" She looked back over her shoulder toward the coat closet.

"What about him?" I said.

"Aren't we taking him with us to the lunch room today?"

"No, he knows the way," I said.

Lizabeth gave me a funny look.

"It was my job to babysit him yesterday," I said, "but today's he's on his own. I've got enough problems to deal with"

Lizabeth looked puzzled, but she didn't say anything. When we got to the cafeteria, I bought a box of milk and deliberately headed off to a table that was already almost full. Lizabeth and I squeezed in, and someone scooted over to let C.J. in after he came through the hot lunch line.

Out of the corner of my eye, I saw Hans stand there for a moment, holding a tray and looking over our way. I was careful not to turn my head, but I saw him walk over to a half-empty table and sit down alone. My stomach unknotted a little when I saw Steve Mates heading off in another direction, with Cliff following him.

I ate my peanut butter and jelly sandwich slowly, and silently told myself not to complain, because a solitary sandwich looked better than today's hot lunch which, although it was called "Italian Delight," looked anything but. Every now and then, I took a peek over at Hans. No one spoke to him while I watched him quietly eating his lunch. I was feeling kind of mad at myself for deserting him, but kept making excuses to myself by thinking I had my own problems to deal with.

The moment we got up, I noticed that Hans untangled his long legs from beneath the cafeteria bench seats and started to follow us. C.J. and Lizabeth headed off to make a stop at the bathrooms, while I went out the cafeteria door. As soon as I was outside, I scanned the playground. There was an empty corner up in the back field that no one was using, and it looked like a good spot to play catch and hit a few balls. I headed that way but hadn't gone far, when Steve and Cliff appeared.

"Well, well, well," Steve said, stepping directly in front of me. "If it isn't Mustard, all on his lonesome." He looked down toward school where Hans was running toward me trying to catch up. "And sure enough, here comes the Nazi to join him." I was glad that Hans was far enough away so that he couldn't hear this latest insult.

I balled up my hands into fists, but I knew I wasn't going to use them. I stared at my feet. I was just glad to be alone so that no one else witnessed this.

Steve turned to walk off, but before he left, he reached up and flipped off my baseball cap just as Hans came running up. The cap fell into the dirt near my feet. Hans quickly bent over to pick it up for me, and Steve took advantage of this target to give Hans a kick in the rear that sent him sprawling face down into the dirt.

C.J. and Lizabeth came running up just in time to see Hans go down.

It was Lizabeth who spoke up. "Get out of here, you two, and leave Hans alone, or I'm reporting you to the yard teacher." She advanced a few steps toward Steve as she spoke.

"Oooh, a little scaredy-cat. Running off to find teacher," Steve taunted.

"Oooh, stupid bully, who's going to find himself in a whole heap of trouble," Lizabeth retorted, turning to look around for the teacher on yard duty who was standing near the climbing apparatus.

"Don't bother. We're out of here," Steve announced. "If we stay here, we're in danger of catching cooties!"

He and Cliff sauntered off. Lizabeth hesitated and then shrugged, probably deciding it wasn't worth reporting them and that it would only embarrass Hans more. By now, he had stood up, brushed himself off, and handed me my cap, looking decidedly puzzled. *"Was ist?"* he muttered. He shook his head. *"Cooties?"*

Lizabeth looked at him helplessly, and then started to giggle. How to explain? Looking at the retreating figures of Steve and Cliff, she finally said, "Dunderheads?"

Hans grinned. *"Dummkopfs.* Ah. *Dunderheads."* He'd added a new word to his vocabulary. That seemed to satisfy him.

I tugged my cap back onto my head. "Want to join us in hitting a few balls, Hans?" I led the way toward the field. It seemed the least I could do after the guy had literally taken the fall for me.

Hans grinned. "Let's step on it," he said.

In a few minutes, I was back in my element, playing ball. It only took a few throws and hits to find out that Hans was a lot better at baseball than basketball. I learned he'd played on one of the Air Force base kids' teams in Germany. In fact, during the next half hour, I made two pleasant discoveries. Hans was really darn good at baseball, and my nose was dripping. Yes, I was sure I was coming down with a cold, which meant I could stay home from school tomorrow!

CHAPTER 4

"**D**on't even bother to get up, Jack," Mom said the next morning when she came in my bedroom to check on me. "I heard you coughing during the night." She put her soft hand on my forehead for a minute. It felt cool. And you've got a little fever, too. Just stay in bed for a while this morning. No school for you today. We're going to nip this cold in the bud."

She had brought with her a bottle filled with some sort of orange-colored medicine and had a spoon in hand. "Take two spoonfuls of this," she said.

I sat up and didn't offer any argument. I took my medicine and quickly fell in with the plan. After Mom left, I snuggled back under the covers and grinned. Sure enough, I'd come down with a cold. For the first time in my life, I was happy about it. No flu or aches and pains, just a plain old head cold with a cough and drippy nose. Now I didn't have to face the bullies who I knew were waiting for me.

At dinner last night, I had complained about my cold a little more than I normally would have. So Mom was already primed to let me stay home for a day and rest up. My cough during the night was enough to convince her.

I dozed off again and didn't even bother to get out of bed until almost ten o'clock when I finally came downstairs for breakfast. Echo came running in from the family room to greet me with frantic tail wagging. I scratched him behind his ears.

Here it was a Thursday morning, and I was still dressed in pajamas, enjoying a second piece of toast and reading the sports pages and all about the upcoming World Series while all my buddies—and the bullies—were at school.

Dad had already left for his job at the IBM plant. Mom only worked part-time at the branch library. Today she worked from eleven to three, and she didn't need to leave our house until around ten-thirty, so she'd fussed about a bit, scrambling an egg for me and making some toast, and now she was getting ready to leave for work. That medicine she'd given me last night and the second dose this morning seemed to help. I wasn't coughing and dripping so much.

Mom finally left the house, after many reminders to "drink lots of liquids," "keep warm," "heat up the chicken soup in the microwave" when I felt hungry, and "be sure to phone" if I needed anything. She insisted that our neighbor, Betty Williams, would drop over to look in on me at one o'clock, even though I said that wasn't necessary, and I'd be perfectly fine at home alone.

Wrapped in a blanket on the couch in the family room, with a big box of tissues and a wastebasket nearby, and with Echo sitting on my feet to keep me warm, I finally had some time to think. How could I avoid having my lunch sack raided by Steve and Cliff every morning? And how could I keep them from mouthing off and calling me and my friends names when no teacher could hear?

I'd already tried taking a different route to school, and that hadn't worked. Today I was safe and snug at home, but I couldn't stay home sick for the rest of the year. Kids weren't allowed to leave school during the lunch hour, so I couldn't walk home to eat and back again. Besides, Mom and Dad were both at work during midday, and they wouldn't want me to come home to an empty house even if I could.

Facing up to the bullies was the clear solution, but getting beaten up wasn't all that attractive, and I'd get in a heap of trouble for fighting at school no matter how the fight started. That didn't stop me from fantasizing a little about secretly learning Tae Kwan Do and then amazing Steve and Cliff with the lightning-quick skill in my feet and hands, but that's all it was, a fantasy.

"I give up, Echo," I said out loud. My dog lifted up his head, and stared at me with his bright brown eyes. He didn't know what was wrong, but he was ready to help. No matter how hard I struggled, I couldn't come up with a good solution.

Finally I abandoned the couch and my bully problem-solving attempts in favor of sitting at the kitchen table and fishing my math homework out of my backpack. Mom had sent me to bed last night right after supper, and I knew I'd have to make up whatever school work I was missing today, so I decided to get it out of the way.

There were twenty word problems, and at least half of them involved dividing fractions. Ugh. But when compared to handling the Steve problem, the math assignment seemed simple. Invert and multiply. I didn't have to know why.

After I polished off the homework, I played some Xbox for a while. Then I got a big drink of water, sat on the couch, pulled up a blanket, and Echo and I watched a little TV. When I got hungry, I heated up the chicken soup and then retreated to the couch again. We were there when Mrs. Williams checked in to see if I needed anything. And we were still there when Mom got home, too.

She immediately gave me more of her magic orange potion, and I got another dose at bedtime. By the time I fell asleep, I was feeling pretty good again. I had stopped coughing, and didn't have a fever. I'd also come up with a plan.

Friday morning I got up earlier than usual and got dressed quickly. I went downstairs, and as I poured myself a bowl of cereal, Echo came to sit at my feet at the breakfast table.

"Hey! What are you doing up so early, Jack?" Dad asked, glancing at his watch. He was usually headed out the door by the time I came downstairs.

"I wondered if you'd give me a ride to school today?" I asked.

"Sure," he said, glancing up at me and looking surprised, "but why do you want to go so early?"

I'd thought this out pretty carefully, so I had an answer ready. "The library's open before school, and I have some books to return and check out. I missed my library period yesterday." What I didn't add was that getting there early and being dropped at the front door meant I wouldn't have to face Steve. I knew this was no long-term solution, buy hey! It might work for today.

And it did work. Dad dropped me off at the front door of Emberley Elementary. I went straight inside and down the hall to the library. I stayed there reading one of the new graphic novels that had come in until the first bell rang. Then I slipped out, and joined my class outside the door of the fifth grade classroom.

As I stood in line, I saw Steve and Cliff come walking up just before the second bell rang. They didn't let on they were surprised to see me, but I knew they were. I quickly turned away and ignored them. I was happy thinking about how they'd been standing out in the far back playground waiting to pounce for me, while I was inside the school all the time.

C.J., Lizabeth, and Hans left the front of the line and came running back to me. I told them about my being sick with a cold yesterday. For Hans's sake, after the explanation, I held a finger in front of my nose, and pretended I had a big sneeze. "Achoo!"

He laughed and said, *"Gesundheit!"*

Lizabeth and C.J. giggled. Then they started filling me in on what I'd missed yesterday. Hans didn't say anything, but he was listening, and he smiled a lot as if he was glad to see me back.

"We're starting an America the Melting Pot unit," Lizabeth said.

"Melting Pot?" What's that all about?" I asked. "A cooking unit? What are we melting?"

"We're not cooking. We're going to study about how people from lots of different countries came to the United States bringing with them customs and holiday foods and words from all over the world. Everyone in the class will pick a country of the world to report on," Lizabeth explained. "We'll write about our country and give an oral report, too."

"Yeah," C.J. continued. "You have to teach the class three words in the language of the country you pick, and explain how they celebrate one of their holidays."

I thought that over for a minute. Didn't sound too bad, except for the oral report part. I didn't like to stand in front of people and talk.

Lizabeth continued, "You can bring in some kind of finger food, like a cookie or cake from your country, or pass around some coins, or a postcard, or anything. We're going to invite our families to come on the night we give our oral reports."

"Last night we were supposed to think about what country we'd like, and we're going to choose them today," C.J. said. "I'm going to pick Italy. That's where my great grandfather lived. What'll you pick, Jack?"

"England, I guess. That's where my great-great-grandparents came from. They lived in the southern part of England, a place called Cornwall. That's where Merlin and King Arthur are from."

"Hey! That'll be a snap," Lizabeth pointed out. "Teaching us three words of English won't be too hard." She laughed.

When the bell rang, we walked inside. Ms. Hollis seemed glad to see me and came right over to ask how I was. As I handed in my math homework, I felt my face getting hot and wondered if she still remembered me blurting out "two brownies" the last time I did a division of fractions problem. If she did, she didn't say anything.

During social studies, Mrs. Hollis walked over to the white erase board and showed the class an alphabetical list of fifty countries. Some of these I recognized, while others I hadn't even heard of. I panicked after I ran my eye down to the "Es" and didn't see England listed.

Almost as if she were reading my mind, Ms. Hollis said, "This is just a partial listing to get us started. I can add to the list any other country you want. I hope you all did some thinking last night about which one you'd like to choose for our Melting Pot Unit. It can be a place from which some of your ancestors came, or it can just be a country that sounds interesting. Since there are so many countries in the world, and so few of us, I want everyone to choose a different country. So, if someone chooses the one you would have liked, you'll need to pick another country, any questions?"

No one said anything.

"Okay," she said. "Who's ready to pick?"

Steve's hand shot up. He wasn't usually quick to raise his hand, so Mrs. Hollis called on him.

"England," he said, "I pick England." He smirked and looked my way. I was positive he'd overheard what I said in line in front of the classroom door when I was talking to C.J. He was only choosing England to stop me from getting it.

"All right," Ms. Hollis said. "You'll notice England isn't on the list. Can anyone tell me why?"

Lizabeth's hand went up, and for about the hundredth time I wondered, is there anything this girl doesn't know?

"The United Kingdom is on your list," Lizabeth said, "and England is part of the United Kingdom."

"Good for you, Lizabeth," Ms. Hollis said. "So Steve, you've chosen the United Kingdom, which includes England, Scotland, Ireland, and Wales. I'm putting the U.K. after your name on my class list," she said as she made a note, "and I'll draw a line through U.K. here on the board since it's no longer available to anyone else."

I didn't bother to raise my hand after that. If I couldn't have England, or the U.K., as Ms. Hollis called it, I really didn't care which country I got. Cliff chose Germany, and I wondered if Steve had put him up to it. I was surprised that this choice didn't seem to bother Mrs. Hollis. I kind of thought she was saving Germany for Hans.

One by one, I heard names of different countries being chosen. China, Japan, and Mexico were quickly snatched up. Lizabeth took France. C.J. took Italy. Finally everyone had made their country selections except for Hans and me.

"What country would you like, Jack?" Ms. Hollis asked.

"Any one is okay," I said, and hoped that came across as willing rather than being totally uninterested.

"All right," she said, "I'm going to choose Switzerland for you. And Hans can work with you on the report. It will be his first big written class assignment, and I'm sure he'll feel more comfortable working with a buddy."

Oh, no, I thought. Here's a perfect example of how something bad can get even worse. Not only didn't I get England, but now I had a country I knew nothing about, and I had to work with somebody. I looked over and saw that Hans had a happy, relieved smile on his face. Maybe he had been worrying about how he'd do a report on his own. I managed to smile back. Working with Hans wouldn't be so bad, and at least I'd have company in my misery.

Ms. Hollis handed out a packet of guidelines in a manila folder to each of us, and she went over some of the stuff with us. We could use books, encyclopedias, magazines, and the Internet to get the information we needed for our written and oral report. We'd get extra credit if we did an interview with someone outside our own family who had lived or traveled in our country.

"Have you ever been to Switzerland?" I whispered to Hans.

"Yah," he said and smiled. With Hans, I was never sure if he was just being agreeable or if he had actually understood what I said. Anyway, it sounded encouraging. My spirits lifted a little. Working with Hans might turn out to be a good thing.

"I've arranged for us to have this next half hour to research in the library, a special extra time for us, so that you can get started on your projects," Ms. Hollis said. "Gather up some paper and a pencil, and here we go on the first leg of our journey to learn about America, the Melting Pot."

Within a few minutes, we were all in the library clutching our packets of guidelines and wondering where to start. Hans, C.J., Lizabeth and I snagged a small round table for four near the back. That prevented any unwanted company from joining us.

"Let's start by finding Switzerland on a map," I said to Hans. I made it sound as if I were doing him a favor by showing him where it was. The truth was, I hadn't the foggiest idea where Switzerland was located, other than somewhere in Europe.

"A map? *Gut*," he answered.

We went over to the reference section where I lifted out a heavy atlas and lugged it back to our table. I looked up Switzerland in the index, and opened the book. "Hey!" I said, as I took my first look. "It's right next to Germany."

"*Yah*," Hans said, grinning. "Here *ist ver* I lived." He pointed to a spot on the map. "Air Force base," he added.

"So you *have* visited Switzerland," I said.

"*Yah, ve* ski there," Hans said.

It was my turn to grin. Not only could Hans play baseball, but he knew how to ski. Come winter here in Colorado, that would sure come in handy. I looked back at the map, and noticed something else.

"Look, you guys," I whispered loudly to C.J. and Lizabeth, both of whom were busy reading in an encyclopedia. "Italy and France are neighbors of Switzerland."

"Uh-huh," Lizabeth said, looking up and then going back to her reading and note taking. Somehow I didn't think my little map facts were news to her. C.J., on the other hand, stopped reading and leaned over to see our map.

"Cool," he said. "Our countries are right next to each other." Apparently his geography was no better than mine.

"Now we need some books," I said to Hans. "We'll put this back first." Hans was quick to pick up the heavy atlas and carried it back to its place.

I could see that Steve and Cliff were hanging around the encyclopedias, and I didn't want to go anywhere near them. So I headed off to a free computer catalog. I typed in Switzerland and was surprised when a lot of books turned up. I wrote down some numbers and Hans and I went to the shelf and each picked a book. I chose one with a lot of pictures so that I could see what the country looked like.

We checked them out, and spent the rest of the period reading and taking notes. I could see that Hans was looking at what I wrote down, so my notes were less scribbled and more complete than usual. Hans began writing things down, too. I glanced over, but I couldn't read what he had written. Maybe they were in German?

When I got to my house that afternoon, I was surprised to find that Dad had come home early. That didn't happen often. He was sitting at his desk with some papers.

"Want to play catch?" he asked when he heard me come in.

"Sure," I said and ran to get my mitt. We were out in the front yard, tossing balls, when out of the corner of my eye, I caught Steve Mates riding by on his bike. He didn't stop or say anything, but he glared at me as if I had no right being there.

At dinner that night, I told mom and dad about the country project and how Hans was going to work with me. "He's been skiing in Switzerland," I boasted. "But we still have to find someone to interview, outside our families, who's lived in or visited Switzerland. That's going to be the hardest part."

"Maybe not," Mom said. "You might be in luck. Remember that house that was for sale around the corner on Judson Street? The house with the yellow door? A couple moved in there this summer. An older man, the father of one of them, I think, lives with them. I'm almost sure Betty Williams told me the older man had come here from Switzerland. Shall I check it out for you?"

"Hey, that would be great, Mom." I remembered the house she was talking about. We both commented when the new owners had painted the door bright yellow.

"I've met the woman who moved in there a couple of times when she was out gardening and I was walking around the block, and I've seen her at the grocery store. I never did really visit. I should have and welcomed them to the neighborhood. Her name is Greta. I'll find out what I can tomorrow morning."

After another dose of the miraculous orange medicine, I went to bed pretty early. All in all, I'd had a good day and the weekend stretched ahead now. But I knew Monday morning would be coming around. I had to have another plan by then.

CHAPTER 5

I was eating breakfast Saturday morning with Echo curled up in
a ball at my feet when the telephone rang. My dad put down
his second cup of coffee and picked up the cordless phone at
the end of the kitchen counter.

"Hey, Max! Good to hear from you," Dad said.

I finished up my cereal and carried my bowl over to the sink,
but hung around because Uncle Max was my favorite uncle, and I
hoped I'd get to talk with him when Dad was finished. Uncle Max
had been a really good baseball player. He had been first baseman
on the local Fairview Knights high school team about fifteen years
ago, the year they won a state championship. In fact, he'd given me
his old first baseman's mitt that had MAX lettered in magic marker
across the back. I used it all the time.

Uncle Max was a good enough player to get a baseball
scholarship to the University of Southern California. From there,
he got the chance to play on the Stockton Ports team in Stockton,
California. He even won a car from the local dealership for being
the team member with the highest batting average. It was a red
convertible, and he drove it out to see us in Colorado and gave me
a ride.

Uncle Max got his big chance when he was finally called up to
play for a California AAA team, the Sacramento River Cats. If he
had done really well, he might have gotten a crack at playing for the
Oakland A's. But he wasn't quite good enough. After one season, he
went back to play at Stockton, and a year after that, he finally quit.
Uncle Max now owned a sporting goods shop in Sacramento. He
had been married, but was divorced now. Mom and Dad always

said he spoiled me, and I guess he did. Whenever I got a package from Uncle Max, I knew it would never be socks or a sweater. It would be something I really wanted.

Dad finally handed the phone to me. "Your Uncle Max has some great news," he said.

"Hi, Uncle Max," I said into the phone.

"Hi, Jack. I knew that you and your dad would be really excited when you found out your Colorado Rockies were going to the World Series."

"We sure are," I agreed. "It's about the best news ever."

"It might get even better," he said.

"Even better?"

"Yeah. How would you like to go down to Invesco Field in Denver and watch one of the World Series games?" Uncle Max said. "Wouldn't that be neat?"

"Oh, wow! " My heart started racing. "Really?" I was afraid I was dreaming and almost pinched myself.

"Really," he said. "One of my old baseball friends owes me a favor. I've phoned him already, and he says he can get me six tickets. Of course I'll feel better when I actually have them in my hands. They aren't even printed yet, but Bill is positive he'll get them. That means you, me, your mom and dad, and two of your friends can go to one of the home games in the Series. It's going to be the same week as your birthday, Jack, so that will be my present to you."

"Oh, wow!" I wasn't often speechless, but at the moment I was pretty close to it. Getting to take my two best friends and go see my Rockies play in a World Series game would definitely be the best birthday party ever.

"I wanted to share the good news with you right away so we can start making plans, even though I'm not certain yet whether our tickets will be for the first or second game they play in Denver. I'll find out on Monday, and I'll call you guys then and make my plane reservations. Okay?"

"Sure!" I said. "Sounds wonderful! Gee, thanks, Uncle Max!" I handed the phone back to my dad before I went running off to find mom and tell her about the tickets.

She had been putting some laundry in the dryer but stopped to hear the good news. "What a tenth birthday you're going to have! One to remember. Birthday dinner is definitely going to be hot dogs at the ball park."

"Yeah! I can't wait!"

I hurried to phone up C.J. "Can you come over after lunch?" I asked him.

"Sure," C.J. said. "What's up?"

I didn't want to spoil the surprise, so I said, "I have a new baseball card I want to show you and Lizabeth, and then I thought we might walk down to the park and hit around a few balls."

"Sounds good. I'll bring my bat and see you at your house around one."

I called Lizabeth next with the same message.

"Great," she agreed. "Why don't you phone Hans and ask him to come, too?"

"No, not this time," I said. "Just you and C.J." I hoped she wouldn't push the Hans issue. It wasn't that I wouldn't want to show Hans my baseball card collection or go to the park with him. But I'd feel kind of funny if the three of them came over, and then I invited only two of them to my birthday party. But, hey! We only had six tickets. C.J. and Lizabeth were my oldest friends, and I'd only known Hans a week.

"Why not ask Hans? I bet he'd love to come." she insisted.

"Not this time," I said.

There was a pause before Lizabeth said, "Okay. I'll be there about one o'clock."

The funny thing was, I really did have a new baseball card to share. I often went on line to sportscardfun.com to find out what cards were available, and sometimes I'd trade or buy one. I kept my baseball card collection in two boxes on a shelf in my closet. I didn't really have that big a collection to brag about yet, but I planned to collect all my life.

Most of my baseball cards were inexpensive Upper Deck cards with members of the Rockies team. I was collecting cards for every one of the forty men on the Rockies roster. And I was trying to get Rookie cards, too. My favorite players this year were Tim Hudson, the first baseman, and George Mathews, the left fielder — and a great hitter. I had just snagged a Rookie card of Mathews for a buck. I was wishing I had one for Hudson too, but they were currently going for twelve dollars, and I wasn't that rich.

C.J. and Lizabeth arrived just a couple minutes apart. I took them to my room and showed them my Mathews. Neither of them collected cards, but they enjoyed looking at mine.

When I thought it was the right moment, I said, "Guess what?"

"What?" C.J. asked.

"I want to invite you both to come to my birthday party."

"Hey! That'll be fun," Lizabeth said. "When is it?"

"I'm not sure of the day yet," I answered.

Lizabeth gave me a funny look. "You don't know what day you'll have your party?"

"I'll know for certain on Monday," I said, "but I just couldn't wait that long to invite you. See, my Uncle Max is getting six tickets to one of the World Series games in Denver. It's a birthday present. Uncle Max, Mom, Dad, me and two of my friends—that's you guys—are going to celebrate my birthday at the park."

"No way!" C.J. jumped up from the bed where he had been sitting. "We're really going to celebrate your birthday at a World Series game?"

"Really," I said.

"Fantastic!" Lizabeth said, as we high-fived all around. "We're going to a World Series game."

"Mom says we'll eat hot dogs at the park," I added. "How perfect is that! And she said she'll call your folks and give them all the details to be sure that it's okay for you guys to have a late night out."

"No problem. My folks will be watching," C.J. said. "Either at our house, or with one of their friends, who has a huge screen. They wouldn't miss it."

"Hey!" Lizabeth added, "wouldn't it be cool if the camera panned across the faces of the fans the way they sometime do on TV, and showed us? Why, we'd be TV stars."

I hadn't considered that possibility. Of course I'd wear my purple-and-white Rockies t-shirt and ball cap. But maybe we should paint our faces or something. I'd have to give some thought to that.

We were all revved up and wished we could go to the game right now, but the next best thing was to head down to the park and play ball.

We all wore our mitts. I took a ball, and C.J. carried his baseball bat. Echo jumped up on each of us, knowing we were going somewhere and wanting to come, too.

"Sorry, boy," I said. "But you have to be on a leash when you're in the park, and I'm going to be busy playing ball today."

I put Echo out in the yard, but I hated the pitiful look he gave me through the patio door. The three of us hurried off to walk the five blocks down to Platt Park. There was a lake in the middle of the park, a playground area with slides and swings in one corner, a recreation center with a pool at the other end, and a sprawling, empty grassy area in between. We headed for the grass.

The three of us took turns. One would pitch, one would hit, and one would field. After five or ten minutes, we'd rotate. Maybe it was because we were so excited about going to a World Series game, but whatever the reason, all three of us were hitting better than usual today.

I was chasing a long fly ball that C.J. had hit over my head when, as I ran, I saw Steve Mates and Cliff heading my way across the grass. My heart started thumping, and it wasn't from running hard. I was scared. What would happen next?

I grabbed up that ball and ran with it toward C.J. and Lizabeth as fast as I could without a glance back in Steve's direction. My hope was that my buddies were still far enough away that they hadn't yet figured out that the rapidly approaching figures were Steve and Cliff. Somehow I had to prevent what I knew would be a humiliating meeting. I didn't want C.J. and Lizabeth to know I was such a coward.

With my mind racing as fast as my feet, I tried to figure out what to do. If only there was some way to get out of here. I couldn't just suddenly say, "C'mon. I've had enough; let's go home." They'd definitely know something was wrong. But if we stayed there and kept playing, Steve and Cliff would soon be upon us. I wasn't sure what they'd do, but I knew it wouldn't be good.

At just that moment from the opposite direction, near the lake, a familiar voice cried out, "Jack, C.J., Lizabeth. Hallo!" It was Hans and he was rushing toward us.

Out of the corner of my eye, I looked back over my shoulder and saw that Steve and Cliff must have heard Hans, too. They had stopped in their tracks.

Hans was not alone. With him was a big high school kid. Both of them came trotting up to us, Hans in front. He grinned.

"*Dies ist* my American *Bruder,* Geoff Collins," Hans said, pointing to the big guy at his side. "Geoff, these my *Freunden,* Jack, C.J., *und* Lizabeth."

"Hi," Geoff said to us. He wore a big smile. "Happy to meet you. Hans talks about you guys all the time. I'm his stepbrother."

"Hi," I said, and C.J. and Lizabeth greeted the newcomers, too.

"Hans tells me you've really helped him in class, and that you're showing him the ropes at recess too," Geoff said.

"No, no," Hans interrupted. "Ve do not play with the jumping ropes. Ve play baseball."

Geoff laughed and shook his head before he explained to Hans that showing someone the ropes simply means showing them how things are done in a new place.

"Ah," Hans said, and I watched him store away another useful expression.

Geoff said, "My family appreciates your help. He's got a lot to learn." Geoff gave Hans a friendly jab in the shoulder.

"Yah," Hans agreed. "*Ich* need somevun to show me the ropes."

"He says you're all baseball fans," Geoff went on. "You must be excited about the Colorado Rockies going to the World Series."

"Yeah," I said, stealing a glance at C.J. and Lizabeth. This was going to be embarrassing when he found out we were going and Hans wasn't.

"We're big fans, too," Geoff said. "Baseball isn't a very big sport in Germany. They're all nuts about soccer, but Hans played a lot of baseball on the school team they had at the Air Force base where my dad was stationed."

"Did you live in Germany, Geoff?" Lizabeth asked.

"No. When my folks split, I stayed here in Boulder with my mom. Dad met Hans's mother while he was stationed in Germany, and they only moved here a couple of weeks ago. I'm a junior at Fairview High this year, and I'm a starter on the baseball team at right field."

"My Uncle Max used to play first base for the Fairview Knights," I said.

"Hey, small world," Geoff said. "My dad's been a Rockies season ticket holder from way back. Even when he was flying back and forth from Germany, he always managed to take in a few games when he was in town. He's going to try to take Hans, and my stepmom and me to one of the World Series games. The season ticket holders get early dibs on seats before they go on sale to the general public."

I exchanged a quick look of relief with Lizabeth and C.J. before I said, "Wouldn't that be great? My dad's hoping to get us some tickets, too. Uncle Max still has some friends from when he played semi-pro ball, and he thinks that one of them might be able to score some tickets for us."

"What are you guys doing here today?" Geoff asked. "Hitting a few balls?"

"Yeah," I said. "We've been doing a little hitting and fielding." As I spoke, an idea struck, and I acted on it immediately. "Why don't you two join us? We could sure use some extra fielders."

Geoff looked at Hans. "Want to play?"

"Yah," Hans said.

And it was as simple as that. The solution to my problem. When Steve and Cliff saw Hans and Geoff with us, they wouldn't try anything.

We started playing, and for a while, I kept glancing back now and then at Steve and Cliff. They stood around for a while, and then when I looked back, they were gone. They must have gotten tired of waiting around.

It was clear at once that Geoff was a fabulous player. When he pitched, he lobbed the ball in nice and easy. When he hit, I had the feeling he was being careful not to knock the ball right out of the park, and he really scrambled out in field and made some impossible catches. Better than that, he kept shouting encouragement to all of us and offering praise. He was not only a star, but a team player as well.

We played for almost two hours before we finally all collapsed on the grass, hot, sweaty, and tired. This was what I called a perfect autumn day!

Geoff finally stood up and thrust his hand into his jeans pocket pulling out some bills. "Great," he said, "I've got a little cash on me. Let's go over to the Rec Center and I'll get us some sodas."

The promise of cold sodas got us up from the grass and over to the Rec Center. I took a good look around but didn't see any sign of Steve. Geoff bought the sodas and a couple of bags of chips to share, and we went back outside and sat in the shade of a tree.

We mostly talked baseball, and I found out that Geoff had a card collection, too. He said he'd show it to me sometime.

Geoff glanced at his watch and said, "Hey, Hans. It's after four o'clock. Time for us to be heading back. Remember, we've got to get ready to go out to dinner tonight."

"Yah," he said with a grin, getting to his feet. "Ve need to step on it."

That made us all chuckle.

"Yeah, we'd better be getting home, too," I said, getting to my feet. "We'll walk up Emerson with you, it's on our way."

We tossed our empty cans in the recycle bin and headed across the street and up the hill. As I walked along next to Geoff, I found myself wishing I had a big brother. He'd probably know exactly what to do about Steve Mates. But unfortunately I didn't, and I'd be facing Steve all alone on Monday morning.

CHAPTER 6

"I phoned Mrs. Stahlein this morning," Mom said. "You know our new neighbor who lives around the corner? When I told her I had a favor to ask, she invited me over. I told her about your school assignment to give a report on Switzerland and how you wanted to do an interview. She said her father, Marcus Schwartz, would be glad to talk with you. He only recently came over to live with them and until then lived in Switzerland all his life."

"That's great," I said. "What's Mr. Schwartz like?"

"I don't know," Mom said. "I didn't get to meet him. He was out with Mr. Stahlein. Mrs. Stahlein said her father doesn't get out a lot. He still feels shy in this new country and is a bit homesick. She thought it would be very good for him to talk with young people. She said he'd be home tomorrow afternoon, and if you'd phone and set a time, he'd be happy to see you and Hans then."

"Tomorrow?" I said, panic rising. *"Tomorrow?* I'm not ready yet, Mom. Hans and I haven't figured out what questions to ask or anything!"

"I'm sure you can think of some excellent questions between now and tomorrow afternoon. I told her there would be two of you, you and Hans, and you'd have to check with him. But I thought you'd want to do your interview right away. You don't have a lot of time on this assignment. Why don't you call Hans and see if he's free tomorrow? If not, you can call Mrs. Stahlein and find another time."

I was still in panic mode when I went to call Hans. How could Mom be so calm about all this? Oh, yeah. She wasn't the one who had to go do the interview!

Hans had given me his phone number, and even though I knew he had said he was going out to dinner tonight, this was an emergency that couldn't wait. I had to call and hoped I'd catch him before he left. I was relieved to find he was still home, and I spilled out the latest developments.

"Could you go with me to do the interview with Mr. Schwartz tomorrow afternoon?" I asked. I was secretly hoping he would say that he had a dentist appointment or something, although that wasn't too likely on a Sunday.

"Yah, sure," Hans said, sounding a little surprised, but eager.

My heart sank.

"Vat time?"

"How about three o'clock?" I said.

"Sure," Hans said. *"Das ist gut."*

"Okay," I said. "I'll phone and tell them we're coming then. Be over here at my house at quarter to three."

"Okay," Hans said. "Vat vill ve ask him?"

"Good question," I said, gnawing on my upper lip and feeling panic again. A very good question, and I had no answer. "I'll work on that tonight," I told Hans. "Okay? And we can talk about it as we walk over."

"Okay," Hans agreed.

How could he be so cool? Oh, yeah. He was counting on me to do all the work. Must be nice to be just be coming along for a free ride.

"Be sure to tell your folks that you'll stay here for a while after the interview so we can start writing the paper. And don't forget your library book about Switzerland," I added. "We may need it."

Then I phoned Mrs. Stahlein and set the interview time for three o'clock. After I hung up, I stood there for a minute, wondering what to do next. It was slowly sinking in. I was going to be doing a big interview tomorrow with perfect strangers, and my only help was going to be Happy Hans. I sighed. It was near dinner time, but I couldn't afford to waste a minute. I had to figure out what to do. I hadn't even cracked open the book I'd checked out of the library, and I didn't have a single intelligent question about Switzerland in my head.

I ran up to my room and quickly pulled out the worksheets that Mrs. Hollis had given us. This time I looked at them seriously. Under "Your Country Report," she had listed History, Geography,

Government, Economy, Folk Tales, Traditions, Food, and Language. The last four looked to me like ones we could ask Mr. Schwartz about. Did he have a favorite folk tale? How did he celebrate one of the traditional Swiss holidays? What was a favorite food? And we sure needed his help in teaching the class three Swiss words or phrases.

On TV and in the movies, I had seen reporters do interviews. They used little notebooks, not like the big three ring notebooks we used at school. I was pretty sure I had one of those little ones somewhere in my desk, not too big but sort of official looking. I found it, black and spiral bound across the top. I opened it to the first page and jotted down "Folk Tale." Then I wrote "Holiday Celebration" on another page, "Recipe" next, and finally "Three words or phrases" on yet another page.

That made me think some more. What would be three good words or phrases? We should have those picked out ahead of time so that Mr. Schwartz could translate them for us. I thought for a minute and then I wrote down, "hello," "thank you very much," and "see you later." That last one was kind of lame, I thought, but maybe Hans would have a better idea. I left space after each one so that there would be room to write the Swiss translation.

At exactly quarter of three on Sunday afternoon, the doorbell rang and I hurried to open it. There was Hans, wearing slacks and a shirt and carrying his library book. Until this moment, I hadn't thought about dressing up for the interview. I was in my usual jeans and an old tee shirt.

"C'mon in," I said, then I took Hans into the living room and introduced him to my mom and dad.

"Hello," both my mom and dad said.

"We've been wanting to meet you, Hans," my mother added. "Please have a seat while Jack gets ready and gets his notebook." She gave me her special look when she said this.

I ran upstairs to my room, taking Hans's library book with me and tossing it onto my desk. I was thinking about the look Mom had given me when she said "gets ready." I knew it meant something. I didn't change my jeans—no point in overdoing things—but I quickly put on a clean shirt, grabbed up my notebook, and rushed back downstairs again. Mom looked at me and smiled.

"C'mon, Hans," I said. "We don't want to be late."

We hurried outside and started on our short walk over to the Stahleins' house. Hans quickened his pace to keep up with me. I was running on adrenalin. I told Hans about the things I thought we should question Mr. Schwartz about, and I shared the list of three words or phrases I had written down. "Does that seem okay?"

"Yah," Hans agreed. "Sounds *gut.*"

I almost growled in frustration. Hans agreed with everything. Didn't he have any ideas of his own? He was going to be absolutely no help at all! It was driving me nuts to have all the responsibility for this interview on my shoulders. But I had to admit that I was glad to have company, even Hans, when we were about to meet strangers.

As we approached the house, I wondered again about their painted yellow door. No one else in the neighborhood had a door painted like that. I wondered if it meant something special, but decided I wouldn't ask about it. Maybe some other time.

I no sooner rang the bell on their porch than the door opened. Clearly they'd been waiting for us. Mrs. Stahlein was a lot older than my mom, but she was about the same size. She had graying blonde hair, and she was wearing a pretty blue dress. She smelled good, too, powder or perfume, I guessed, and it made me glad that I'd changed my shirt.

"I am Greta Stahlein, and this is my father, Marcus Schwartz," she said as she brought us into the room.

A small old man, with thinning hair, struggled to get to his feet and smiled at us as he said, "Hallo," and gave a little bow with his head.

"I'm Jack Tresidder," I said, "and this is my friend, Hans Ollig."

We both shook hands with Mr. Schwartz. His hands felt cold and dry.

"I thought we'd sit at the table and enjoy some cake and milk while we visit," Mrs. Stahlein said. "It will be easy that way for you to take notes."

I noticed that Mr. Schwartz used a cane when he walked over to the table. Still, he managed to stand tall and proud. He wasn't bent over or anything. We were all busy for the next few minutes as Mrs. Stahlein poured out glasses of cold milk for us, and cups of tea for her father and herself. Then she cut slices of the cake and served them on little plates. The cake looked delicious, and I couldn't resist taking a quick bite. It was nutty and chocolatey.

"Umm, very good," I said, being careful to wipe my mouth with a napkin that had been folded and placed right next to my plate. It was hard not to take another bite, but I couldn't very well ask questions with a full mouth.

"Thank you," Mrs. Stahlein said, and she smiled. "I'm glad you like it."

I flipped open my notebook and tried to look official. "I think my Mom told you, we're making a report on Switzerland, and I have four questions I'd like to ask you, Mr. Schwartz. First, do you have a favorite folk tale or story that kids in Switzerland like to read?"

Mr. Schwartz looked at me with bright brown eyes, but didn't say a word. For a moment, I wondered if he had trouble hearing, but before I embarrassed myself by asking my question again in a much louder voice, Mrs. Stahlein began speaking to him in a foreign language. Swiss, I guess. Only then did I realize that this interview was going to be a lot harder than I had expected. Apparently, Mr. Schwartz didn't speak English.

After Mrs. Stahlein spoke for a bit, Mr. Schwartz answered her, and then she said, "Papa says that he thinks the most famous of the Swiss folktales is the story of William Tell."

"Oh," I said, with a rush of relief. "William Tell. I've heard of him. He's the guy who shot an apple off his son's head, isn't he?"

"Yes, that's right," Mrs. Stahlein said, and she quickly said something to her father. He laughed and looked pleased that I knew the story. I was pretty proud of myself.

I quickly jotted this down in my notebook and turned the page over to holiday celebration. "How do you celebrate one of your holidays, like Christmas, in Switzerland?"

Mrs. Stahlein smiled and said a few words to her father.

"*Ah, schone Wienachten,*" Mr. Schwartz said.

"*Ya, frohliche Weihnachten,*" said Hans. And to my astonishment, Hans and Mr. Schwartz began talking to one another. No interpreter needed, thank you. In fact, they went on for so long, with Mrs. Stahlein smiling, commenting, and nodding her head now and then, that I began to feel left out. I made the most of this time though by taking a drink of milk and eating my slice of cake. Boy, it was good, filled with nuts and chunks of chocolate.

"I didn't know you spoke Swiss, Hans," I managed to squeeze into a short pause in the conversation. "You should have told me." Didn't he realize how much I'd been sweating this interview and how much more comfortable I'd have been if I knew Hans spoke Swiss?

"Swiss?" Hans said. "No, I talk German to Mr. Schwartz."

Puzzled, I turned to Mrs. Stahlein. "Do you speak German as well as Swiss?" I asked.

"There is no Swiss language," Mrs. Stahlein explained. "The Swiss people speak Romansh, Italian, French, or German depending on which part of Switzerland is their home. Where Papa lived, people speak Swiss-German. We read things written in German, but when we talk, our Swiss-German is a little different from regular German. Many of us speak Swiss-German, German, and English."

So nobody in Switzerland spoke Swiss. How dumb could I be? I was saved from being too embarrassed, though, because the three of them were so busy jabbering away in German and enjoying themselves that no one paid any attention to my goof. I wasn't sure who looked happiest at having found someone to talk to, Mr. Schwartz or Hans.

Hans finally turned to me and said, "In your *Buch*, write, Mr. Schwartz has Christmas tree. *Und der ist* sweets *und* presents. Much the same as Germany," he added.

"Is there a Santa Claus?" I asked.

"*Ja. Sankt Nikolaus*," Hans said, while at the same time, Mr. Schwartz said, "*Samichlaus.*" They both smiled.

Hans looked at my notebook. "Vat else did ve vant to ask?"

"We need to bring in some kind of food to taste," I said. "Cake or cookies, or something. So we need a recipe."

"You seem to like this Tiroler cake," Mrs. Stahlein said, as she served me a second piece. "I'd be happy to give you the recipe. Or if you like, I could bake one for you to take to school. It's a very common dessert in Switzerland, and Papa's favorite."

"That would be wonderful," I said, "but wouldn't that be way too much work for you?" I knew that it must take a lot of time and work to make a cake as fancy and good as the one I'd been eating.

"No," Mrs. Stahlein said, giving a little brushing motion of dismissal in the air with her hand. "No problem at all. Papa is always happiest when I have an excuse to bake a cake. He has a real sweet tooth."

"*Sweet tooth?*" asked Hans, clearly puzzled.

"Having a sweet tooth means you like cake, candy, and sweet things," I explained, feeling a little better that I could teach someone something. And I watched Hans add yet another phrase to his vocabulary.

"You tell me the date and time, and you shall have a cake," Mrs. Stahlein said.

I was beginning to like this Melting Pot assignment more and more.

"The only other thing we wanted," I said, "was to translate three words or phrases from English into Swiss... I mean into Swiss-German," I corrected myself, "to teach our class."

"This will be a good test for Papa," Mrs. Stahlein said. "You say it in English, Jack, and we'll see if Papa understands and can give you the Swiss-German. Hans can write it down."

"*Ja,*" Hans said.

Mrs. Stahlein turned and spoke a few words to her father.

Hans took my notebook and pencil.

In English, I said, "Hello."

Mr. Schwartz replied, "*Gruezi,*" and Hans wrote that in my notebook.

"Thank you," I said.

"*Merci vilmal,* Thank you very much," responded Mr. Schwartz.

"See you later," I said.

Mr. Schwartz, looked puzzled, and finally said, "Greta?"

"*Bis spoter,*" said Mrs. Stahlein. Then she translated, "See you later. And indeed I hope we do," she added.

Hans handed the notebook back to me. "*Das ist alles,*" he said.

"That's all?" asked Mr. Schwartz. He sounded disappointed.

"Yes," I said, "you've been a great help and have answered all our questions. The day we give our report, family and friends will be invited to come to the school. We'd like to invite you to come that day."

"We'd love to," Mrs. Stahlein said, and she translated to her father.

"*Ja,*" he said, smiling and nodding.

Before we left with promises of visiting again, Mrs. Stahlein wrote out the recipe for the cake. Hans wrote down his mother's name, telephone number, and address. I felt sure Mrs. Stahlein would soon be in touch with Mrs. Ollig.

As we walked back to my house, I said to Hans, "That was fun, partner," and poked him in the shoulder.

"Partner?" He looked puzzled.

"Yeah. Partner, friends, buddies. We're going to have the best report in class." I thought for a minute and realistically added, "Or, at least as good as Lizabeth's.

Hans grinned back at me and said, "*Ja*, buddy," and gave me a little poke in the shoulder.

CHAPTER 7

After leaving Mrs. Stahlein and Mr. Schwartz, Hans and I walked the short distance back to my house. I was feeling good. We'd gotten all the answers to our questions and were guaranteed a good report. Oh, all right, I'd admit that ours might not be as well written as Lizabeth's. Of course hers would be perfect. But the Tiroler cake samples would make our report really popular. I could already picture in my head the smiles of approval from everyone in class as Hans and I finished giving our report on Switzerland.

But between now and that happy moment of applause from an audience bowled over by our brilliance and especially by Mrs. Stahlein's baking, there was the little matter of actually writing the report. We had to get started. When we reached my house, I paused at the foot of the stairs to yell to Mom, "We're home! Everything went just fine." Then Hans and I thundered upstairs to my room.

Echo chased right behind us, tail wagging hard, as if he hadn't seen me for days.

"Do you boys want a snack?" Mom called from the kitchen.

"Thanks, Mom, but we've already had one," I called down.

Up in my room, I sat at the computer and Hans pulled up a chair close to me. On the blank screen, I typed "Switzerland" and beneath that "by Jack Tresidder and Hans Ollig." Then I typed "Introduction." So far, so good. It was looking great. But what next? I paused and looked at Hans. He smiled sort of blankly.

"Mrs. Hollis told us exactly what she wanted in the report on those work sheets she handed out," I said. "They can be our outline."

I picked up the school folder and showed Hans where Mrs. Hollis had listed history, geography, government, economy, folk lore, traditions, food, and language. I typed in each of those as headings down the left side of the report, leaving some space after each one.

"Now, all we have to do, "I said cheerfully, "is fill it in."

Hans smiled encouragingly but still said nothing.

"See, here under folk lore, I'll type, 'A favorite Swiss folk tale is the story of William Tell.' Then in just a few words, we should write a little about that story because some kids in the class won't know it."

"I don't remember the story too vell," Hans admitted. "Just that he shoot the arrow at the apple and miss his son's head."

"Yeah, but I think there's more to it," I suggested. "We'll use good old Google." Within moments we'd found the folk tale and read it off the computer screen. Then we worked together to type in a sort of summary until we were both happy with it.

"See?" I said. "That part is done."

"Ya," Hans said, as he smiled and gave a little sigh of relief. We paused to give ourselves high-fives.

"Is a *gut* beginning," Hans said, nodding his head.

We went on like this to put in information under "Traditions" about how Mr. Schultz said he celebrated Christmas. Hans read from my notes which were in English and from his which, I guess, were in German. A least I couldn't understand his scribbles. Then I'd type things in.

Under "Food," I typed in the recipe for a Tiroler cake that Mrs. Stahlein had given me, and finally under "Language," I put in the three phrases that Hans had written down that we were going to teach the class in Swiss-German.

At this point, I saved what we had written so far on the computer and did a spell-check. Lots of red showed up, showing I'd misspelled more than a few words, but they was pretty easy to click and correct.

"Now," I said, feeling pretty good about how much we'd accomplished so far, "we can read our library books to get some of the other stuff. Why don't we start with history? It comes first in the outline. Look in your book and see what you can find."

"Ya," Hans said. He got his book, and I took mine, and we started thumbing through pages and reading stuff. Hans sat in his chair near my desk, while I flopped down on my stomach on my bed. It was my favorite way to read. It might seem a little strange, but I really think best while laying on my stomach. Echo curled up right next to me.

I'd been reading for about ten minutes, flipping pages and scanning for information, when I noticed Echo got up and jumped off the bed. That was odd. I glanced over at Hans and noticed he wasn't turning pages. Instead, he was sitting there, looking straight ahead, and gently rubbing Echo's ear. I waited a bit, but Hans didn't go back to reading. He continued to pet Echo.

"What's up?" I asked.

"Nothing," he said, glancing toward me before quickly turning away, but I was pretty sure before he turned his head that I'd seen tears in the corners of his eyes.

"Something wrong?" I asked, sitting up and dangling my legs over the bed.

Hans sniffed and dragged a hand across his face. "No," he said. "Talking in German to Mr. Schultz, and now these pictures. They make me a little, how you say it, *house sick?* Some of them look just like my old village, *und* I miss it."

"Homesick," I corrected him automatically. Then I wasn't sure what else to say, so I didn't say anything. I mean, I had known he was the new kid, and all, but until now I hadn't really thought about what that meant. I'd been so busy pitying myself for being bullied by Steve and Cliff that I hadn't thought about how Hans might feel as a total stranger here. Echo had picked up on those homesick vibes a whole lot faster than I did. I knew my dog always snuggled in a little closer to me whenever I felt bad.

"I find some *gut* information," Hans finally said. He sat up, grabbed his book, and started slowly reading aloud some sentences to me.

I was relieved that the awkward moment was over.

"I found some things, too," I said. "Why don't you do the typing this time, under History?"

Hans hesitated. "I don't spell too vell in German," he admitted, "*und* even worse in English."

"No problem," I said. "I'll help, and we've got spell-check!"

Hans seemed to brighten up, as we each shared the facts we'd found, and he typed. We'd turned up quite a bit of information. Some of his sentences were a bit strange, but I helped smooth them a little. Between us, we got some of the history things out of order, too, but we moved sentences around until pretty soon, we had a decent page on the history of Switzerland.

"Enough!" I yelled jumping up. "Time to quit for the day." Hans was careful to save on the computer what we'd written so far.

"I vish I rode my bike over," Hans said, as we walked downstairs.

"I haven't ridden mine for a long time, " I confessed. "My bike's not working. I'm not too good at fixing things, and I keep forgetting to remind Dad about it. The chain's all screwed up. I haven't ridden it for a month."

"Hey!" Hans said. "I'm *gut* mechanic. I take a look for you?"

"Sure," I said. I'd take any help I could get. I was definitely not Mr. Fix It.

We went out to the garage, and I quickly saw that Hans really knew what he was doing. He looked at the bike, checked out the tools on my Dad's workbench that was in the back corner, and within half an hour, my bike was fixed.

"Thanks," I said, sitting back and admiring what he had done. My purple bike, with its little license plate at the back that read "Jack," was ready to go.

Hans was his usual cheerful self by the time he left.

By Monday morning, I had a new plan to try against the bullies, and I was ready to put it into action. I had hatched it last night before falling asleep. I didn't know if it was a good idea or not, but it was the best I could come up with.

I finished my breakfast, and my father had already left for work when I said, "I'm going to ride my bike to school today, Mom."

"Really?" It was another late morning start for my mother. She didn't go into the library to work today until ten o'clock, so she was enjoying a second cup of coffee and reading the newspaper. She dipped down the pages and looked up over them to say, "I thought you said days ago that you were having trouble with the chain on that bike and had sort of given up on it."

"Yeah, I had," I admitted, "but it's fixed now. Before he went home yesterday, Hans worked on it."

"That new friend of yours is pretty handy, isn't he?" Mom said.

"Sure is," I agreed.

A few minutes later, I was on my bike whizzing toward school. Everything was working fine, and I enjoyed riding again. I was kind of ashamed I'd let it go so long. My dad would have helped me fix it, but he'd been working late a lot, and I hadn't mentioned it to him. I hated to ask for help. and I didn't try to fix it on my own. Oh, I liked to tinker and take things apart, all right. The problem was, when I put them back together, I always had a few extra pieces.

The bike racks were near the front of the school, near the teachers' parking lot. I timed it so that I'd arrived just before the first bell rang. I felt nervous as I sat there looking over my shoulder. But no one appeared. After locking up my bike in the rack, I hurried around to our classroom door as the bell was ringing and the kids were starting to line up. I quickly joined Lizabeth, C.J. and Hans, while keeping an eye open for Steve and Cliff. Sure enough, they rounded the building from the playground side and walked over and got in line. I could feel their eyes on me.

"Did you ride your bike today?" Hans asked.

"Yeah," I said.

"*Und*, how did it verk?"

"Great," I said, and told C.J. and Lizabeth that Hans was a terrific mechanic.

During social studies that morning, when Mrs. Hollis gave one of her usual friendly reminders about hoping we were all at work on our Melting Pot reports, instead of trying to slink down in my seat out of sight and avoiding her eye because I hadn't even started on the project, I held up my head, looked over at Hans, and we both grinned. For a change, I was not the great procrastinator.

During P.E., baseball was on everyone's mind. With the World Series coming, who could be thinking of anything else? The student teacher took ten kids and headed up to the far field to practice pitching, throwing, catching, and hitting. The rest of us got to play a game. Mr. Rhoads, the P.E. teacher, chose two captains, Lizabeth and Cliff, and the captains took turns picking players for their team. Of course C.J., Hans, and I all ended up on Lizabeth's team with a lot of girls, while Cliff first picked his buddy, Steve, and then, one by one, the best players in the class. I wasn't feeling any too good about the probable outcome of this game and the way Steve would be crowing over his team's victory.

One of the boys picked for Cliff's team started to give him a hard time. The boy wanted to play second base instead of going to the outfield. I watched as Steve trotted up to the boy and said, "Are you giving my buddy a hard time?" The boy backed down and headed for the outfield. Then before he headed over to third base, Steve gave Cliff a friendly punch in the shoulder.

We launched into a game. Our team was up first, and we quickly made a couple of runs. After three outs, we took to the field. I played first base, my favorite position. Lizabeth was shortstop, and Hans and C.J. were in the outfield. We had a pretty good couple of innings with lots of hits. We were in the top of the third inning, and the score was tied with one out. Hans was on third base. I was up at bat. On the second pitch, I hit a really long fly ball. I headed for first while Hans tagged up at third and waited to see what happened. Sure enough, the center fielder caught my ball for the second out. But Hans easily scored.

Our pitcher was good, and in the bottom of the third, we had two outs when Steve came up to bat. Clearly he was swinging away, hoping for a home run. Too anxious, he reached for a low, outside ball and hit a grounder into the infield. He barreled towards first. Lizabeth scooped up the ball and threw it to me. I caught it, stepped on the bag, and moved slightly toward second, grinning, proud of the play, and totally happy that Steve was out.

I looked toward home plate. Steve was just a few feet away. He wasn't slowing down. He looked like a big, old rhino charging at me with a determined look in his eyes. I wanted to run away. But a first baseman stands his ground. And I was a first baseman.. A good one. Steve might steal my brownies, but he wasn't going to run me off the ballfield. Instead of running straight ahead or to the outside of the base path, Steve veered slightly and headed straight at me. He rammed into my left side. I flew back and hit the dirt. Somehow, I hung onto that ball. I don't know why that seemed important, but it did.

Mr. Rhoads came running over. "Steve! What were you thinking? Are you okay, Jack?"

"Sure," I said as I got up, dusted myself off, trying to look nonchalant even though I had to resist the urge to look around carefully to see if any of my body parts had fallen off. I hurt all over.

Mr. Rhoads said, "You owe Jack an apology, Steve."

Steve hesitated.

"Now!" Mr. Rhoads said.

"Sorry," Steve muttered, and then turned and walked off.

Mr. Rhoads glanced at his watch. "Good game. Time to head on in."

We'd won! It wasn't a regulation game or anything, but we'd won. Hans, C.J. Lizabeth and some of the other players first crowded about to make sure I was okay. When they saw I may have been bruised but not broken, they clapped me on the back. All of us on Lizabeth's team whooped it up a bit as we ran back through the playing field to the outside gym door.

Back in class, there were a few announcements and reminders, and it was time to go home.

C.J., Lizabeth, Hans and I all walked out front toward the bike rack. I had more than a few aches and bruises that I wasn't talking about and was secretly glad that instead of walking, I could ride home today—that is, if my left leg could pedal. We were so busy talking, that at first I didn't notice anything unusual.

It was Hans who first said, "Look!" He pointed at my bike. Both the tires were flat.

Then I heard a little snickering behind me over at the sidewalk at the end of the building. It was Steve and Cliff. They saw me look their way and didn't bother to disguise the smirks on their faces. No doubt about it. Those two had let the air out of my tires and had been waiting for me to find their dirty work.

"Hey, too bad," C.J. said to me, completely unaware of what had really happened. "You haven't been riding for quite a while. I guess you must have a slow leak in your tires."

"Both of them?" Lizabeth said. "Bad luck."

I saw Hans glance over at Steve and Cliff who were just starting to walk off, laughing at something. Hans looked a little puzzled and maybe a bit suspicious, but he said nothing. No doubt he was remembering that the last thing we had done yesterday after he fixed the bike was to pump up the tires. Of course there could have been a leak. But I'd checked both tires this morning and knew they were fine when I came to school.

We started home together, each of my buddies dropping off as we came to their street, and with me walking my bike. I tried putting up a good front as if nothing was wrong. When the last one had dropped off, and there was no one to see, I started limping. It was hard to deny the pain in my left leg. Somehow I kept thinking that if I didn't talk about this bullying in any way, even to myself, it wasn't really happening.

It wasn't until I was a few doors from home that I admitted not only was my leg hurting, I felt sick. Sick to my stomach. Another bright idea of mine had failed.

CHAPTER 8

When Mom saw me limping in from the garage, I explained to her that I'd taken a fall on the baseball field. That was true enough. Of course, I didn't go on to say I'd been deliberately run over by a human bulldozer who hated me and stole parts of my lunch on a regular basis.

"Honey, you have plenty of time before dinner," Mom said. "You go right on up and take a good hot bath. It'll make you feel lots better."

As I sat soaking, I did some hard thinking about my problem. Actually, the problem that faced me was simple enough. It was the solution that was hard to see. How could I avoid having my lunch sack raided by Jack and Cliff every morning? Or watch Steve and Cliff get away with letting the air out of my bike tires? How could I stop the bullying?

I'd already tried taking a different route to school and entering the playground from the far side. That hadn't worked. I couldn't regularly catch a ride in the car with my dad, because he'd want to know why I suddenly wanted to get to school so early every day. I couldn't very well tell him it was because I was a coward who couldn't face up to bullies. Riding my bike would get me to school, but obviously as I'd found out today, there were a couple of problems with that. And if I rode regularly to school, they'd wise up soon and wait for me at the bike racks.

Finally, another idea hit me. I wouldn't carry a lunch sack. If I didn't have one, Steve and Cliff couldn't raid it. I'd buy a hot lunch, as simple as that. By the time I climbed out of the tub and toweled off in the bathroom, not only did my leg feel better, but my mind felt better, too. I pulled on my clothes, and with the side of my hand, rubbed clean a spot on the steamed-up mirror so that I could see to comb my hair. I wished problems could be cleared away that easily.

I might face a few questions from Mom about why I suddenly wanted to buy the cafeteria lunch, but not many. They posted a menu in the local paper, and I could tell her it sounded pretty good so I wanted to give it a try. I knew she'd actually be pleased. I could remember how many times she'd tried to convince me to buy a good hot lunch, and how discouraged she'd become when I refused. She'd think it was practically a miracle that I was willing to give it a try this year. Of course if I bought lunch, I'd have to eat it. Ugh! But that would be a small price to pay to avoid being bullied every morning.

After dinner that night, before I went up to bed, I checked in the school newspaper, and then sprang my idea on her.

"They're serving pizza for hot lunch tomorrow, Mom. Sounds good. Is it okay if I give it a try?"

Mom's face first expressed surprise and then delight. "Of course," she said. I think she wanted to say more about what a good idea it was, but she held herself in check, not wanting to scare me off.

Tuesday morning with money for hot lunch tucked in my jeans pocket, I set off for school. I had a pretty good-sized bruise, but my leg wasn't hurting much. I took my normal route, and as I approached the opening in the fence onto the school grounds at the back of the playing field, I saw the all too familiar figures slouched there, waiting. They must have caught sight of me at the same time, because I saw them both straighten up. My heart rate probably doubled, even though I'd been expecting them. I was careful not to slow my pace while my stomach was doing flip-flops.

As I passed through the gate, Steve quickly stepped in front of me to block my way, while Cliff came around to the rear. "What happened to your bike, Mustard?" Steve demanded. He had a silly satisfied smirk on his face.

"Decided to walk today," I said shortly and tried to move on by.

"Stand where you are," Steve growled, and I stood still while Cliff untied the flap on my backpack, managing to jerk me around as he pulled on the straps.

"Nothin' here," Cliff said after a minute of feeling around.

"What's up, Mustard?" Steve demanded.

I tried to look innocent. "What do you mean?"

Steve poked his index finger hard into my chest just below the shoulder blade to emphasize each word as he asked, "Don't get cute with me. Where's your lunch?"

"I didn't bring a lunch," I said. "They're serving pizza today, and I'm buying hot lunch."

"Really?" Steve said. "I don't think so. Empty your pockets."

I turned out one pocket which had nothing in it except a package of gum. Cliff took that.

"The other one," Steve demanded.

I turned out the other pocket and there was my lunch money. Steve took the two dollars and change and shoved it into his own pocket.

"Hey! You can't do that," I protested.

"And who's going' to stop me?" asked Steve, leaning into my face.

I just stood there.

"Later, Mustard," he said as he and Cliff walked off.

Disgusted with myself, I headed off to the fifth grade wing to get in line outside the classroom door. What had I been thinking? Did I really believe I could solve my problem that easily? It was as easy for Steve to take money as a brownie.

While I stood there in line, I only half-listened as Lizabeth, Hans, and C. J. relived a little of the glory of yesterday's baseball game. They were still glowing over our victory, but that moment of triumph had completely faded away as far as I was concerned. All joy had been lost in my latest defeat. In fact, I couldn't imagine ever being happy again.

As usual, the first thing Mrs. Hollis did was take roll and hot lunch count. I didn't raise my hand for a hot lunch. I could have charged it. My school lets you do that, but eventually that would take explaining about what had happened to my lunch money. I didn't like to lie and say I'd lost it, but even worse would be to say I'd let two bullies take it away from me. I checked to see and found that I had a couple of quarters in my desk. Not enough for lunch, of course, but I could buy a box of milk.

All this was weighing on my mind so I didn't get too excited when Mrs. Hollis said she'd arranged a special extra library period for us to go and work on our Melting Pot reports.

"I hope you're all working hard on your country reports," Mrs. Hollis said. "They'll be due in another week. I can hardly wait to hear them."

"*Gut,*" Hans whispered to me. "Ve get more done."

He wore a happy grin on his face that made up for my lack of enthusiasm.

"Yeah," I agreed, and managed a half-hearted smile.

In the library, the four of us snagged the same table that we'd used last time. I had the manila folder that Mrs. Hollis had given us along with a print-out of what we'd written so far. Looking back at the outline, I said to Hans, "The next thing we need to tackle is geography."

"A map?" Hans said.

I brightened at that. Here was Hans actually volunteering an idea of his own.

"Yeah," I agreed. "We should probably draw a map to show where Switzerland is and what its neighbors are, and maybe we can put some stuff on it like rivers and lakes."

We both walked over to the spot where the big Atlas was. Why wasn't I surprised when just before we got to the table where it rested, Steve rushed in from the other direction and grabbed it. Sheesh! Did that guy just hang around seeing what I wanted to do next so that he could get in my way?

"You guys weren't planning to use this, were you?" he whispered, as he hauled it off toward his table, chuckling a little as he went. "I'm afraid that I'm going to be looking in it for a long, long time."

Hans looked disappointed.

"Hey!" I said. "No problem." I wasn't going to let Steve stomp out Han's first big idea to add to our report. "There are lots of maps around."

By this time I knew that books on Switzerland were filed under 914.94, and there were several of them. I led the way through the shelves and Hans followed. Once in the right spot, we browsed in a couple of the books and found maps in almost every one of them.

Hans grinned. "I like dis vun," he said. "Is *gut.*" He pointed at a page.

"Okay," I said, "and I'll look in this book to find some information about their mountains and lakes."

I soon learned that Hans had yet another talent that I hadn't known about. Along with linguist and mechanic, I could add artist, or at least map-maker, to his growing list of skills. Hans looked at the map in the book and it didn't seem hard for him at all to draw it freehand on a piece of plain white paper. I would have had to trace it, but not Hans. In no time at all, he had the outline of Switzerland and the countries immediately around it and was starting to write in a few of the key cities. He was using a black felt pen, and his drawing looked professional.

What happened next was my fault, really. I should have been more alert, but I got so interested in admiring the map Hans was making that I forgot all about keeping an eye on Steve. Before I knew what happened, Steve and the big atlas he was carrying came crashing down onto our table, hitting Hans's shoulder and arm.

Hans's arm got knocked across the sheet of paper, and an ugly black felt mark swept across the whole page of the beautiful map he'd been working on.

"Ooooh. So sorry," Steve said. "Did I ruin your pretty picture?"

Ms. Anderson, the librarian, came rushing over. "Are you all right?" she asked Hans.

Hans sat up and rubbed his shoulder. "Ya," he said. "But my map is not so *gut*."

"Oh, dear," she said. "Well, I'm glad you're not hurt."

Then she turned to Steve. "Really, Steve, you must be more careful when you're carrying such a heavy book. You could have really hurt someone. And what were you doing with the atlas over here anyway?"

"Sorry," Steve said, bowing his head. "I thought Jack wanted it next."

I had to give him credit. He was doing a pretty good acting job of looking very sad.

"I'll put the atlas away and I'll be more careful," Steve added.

After Ms. Anderson turned and left, Steve dropped his "sorry" face as he said to Hans with a grin, "Tough luck."

Lizabeth and C.J. leaned across the table to assess the damage.

"Too bad," C.J. said. "It was looking neat."

"Yeah," Lizabeth agreed. "You're really good at drawing maps, Hans."

Hans looked up at the clock.

"No time to do it all again, I think," he said, looking sad.

I was boiling over inside. Steve had gotten away with it again. He wasn't the least regretful of the damage he'd caused. Yesterday, he'd knocked me flat. Today, it was poor Hans. And all Steve every got was a 'be more careful warning.'

At that point, Ms. Anderson came bustling back to our table, and she was carrying something small in her hand.

"What a pity that your good work was spoiled in that accident," she said to Hans. "I'm so sorry, and I'm wondering if we might be able to save it. Here's some white-out. Let's just see if we can cover up that ugly line that's spoiling your map. Jack, may I sit there in your seat for a moment?"

"Sure," I said, jumping out of the way.

Ms. Anderson sat down in my seat next to Hans, and unscrewed the bottle of white-out. She pulled out of the bottle the small white sponge stick that was covered with white liquid, and she neatly painted with the sponge generously covering up the jagged line. Then she blew on the page a bit to speed the drying before she added a second coat of white-out.

"There!" she said looking satisfied and standing up. "It's almost invisible."

Hans looked a little dubious. True, the jagged line was gone, but now a long white raised streak crossed his map. It was far from the perfect drawing he had started out with.

"*Danke*, thank you," he said politely.

"Oh, we aren't finished yet," Mrs. Anderson said. "Come with me, boys."

Exchanging puzzled looks, Hans and I followed Ms. Anderson to the little glassed-off office that was located right behind the check-out stand.

She put the map sheet on the copy machine, pressed a button, and out came a page on the printer with Han's map looking as good as new.

"What do you think?" she asked, picking it up and looking at it.

"It's perfect," I said. "No sign of that line."

"Ya," Hans agreed.

"Or would you like it a little larger so that it would be easier to print the names of more cities on it?" she asked.

Hans looked at me and we both nodded.

Ms. Anderson took the map, went back to the copier, pressed a few more buttons and out came the map again, sharp, clear and twice as big as before. This time she'd made two copies.

"There you go," she said. "Problem solved."

Hans and I took the two maps back to our table and showed them to C.J. and Lizabeth. I think they were almost as happy as I was.

In the few minutes we had left, Hans set right to work, adding more cities to the map while I took notes about major mountains, rivers and lakes. Every now and then, though, I made sure to glance over at the table where Steve and Cliff were sitting. Steve caught my eye once and glared at me.

"Maybe you can stop at my house after school tonight," I suggested to Hans, "and write the names of the rivers and lakes on our map."

"*Gut* idea," he agreed.

I was so pleased with the way the map fiasco had worked that I had almost forgot until we lined up to go to the cafeteria that I didn't have any lunch.

When we got to the lunch room, I peeled off and bought a carton of chocolate milk, and then went to find Lizabeth and Hans at a table. C. J. soon joined us carrying his hot lunch. By gosh, that pizza looked pretty good. It probably tasted like cardboard, but it looked and smelled okay.

I pulled open my milk carton and took a drink.

"Where's your lunch?" Lizabeth asked.

Fortunately, I'd had plenty of time to prepare for this question. "Home on the counter," I lied. "Forgot to put it in my backpack."

"You can charge a hot lunch," C.J. offered.

"Naw," I said. "This milk will be okay, and I'll have a snack when I get home."

Lizabeth sounded just like my mother when she said, "Jack, you can't go all day without something inside you." She began rummaging in her lunch box. "Let's see, what I've got here."

"Hey, I can't eat your lunch," I protested.

"Don't worry, you're not going to," she replied. "I'm only going to give you the most undesirable bit." She grinned when she said this. "Not either one of my two-bite brownies," she went on, "or my chips." She set these on a napkin close to her. "But, how about a tasty and healthful clementine?"

She gave it to me with a smile, and I took it.

"And my carrot sticks and celery are all yours," C.J. added, handing them over before he picked up his pizza slice.

Hans didn't say anything, but he handed over the small half of his cheese sandwich which was on thick homemade bread.

Sitting there, feasting among my buddies, I felt a lot better. That is until I had that strange sensation that someone was staring at me. You know the creepy feeling. I looked around. Sure enough, there was Steve, boring holes in my back. When he caught my eye, He raised high a piece of pizza he'd bought with my money, held it out toward me, and then quickly brought it back in toward him and took an enormous bite.

What could I do tomorrow?

CHAPTER 9

A s we walked home from school, I said to Lizabeth and C.J.,
"Hans and I are going to work at my house on our
Switzerland report this afternoon. You guys want to come
over, too, and work on yours? Mom baked brownies."

"Sure," C.J. immediately said. I've never known C.J. to turn
down anything sweet to eat.

"I've been working on my Italy report with my reading teacher,"
he went on. "I'm supposed to have a final draft for her tomorrow. It's
been kind of a grind finishing it up. I'd love some company."

"And you love brownies," I teased.

He grinned back at me.

"Yeah, I'll come over. Sounds good," Lizabeth agreed. "But I
have to go home first and collect some stuff."

"Me, too," said C.J.

"Yah, I go home first, too," said Hans.

By three-thirty, everyone had re-gathered in our kitchen.
Mom put a plate of brownies on the table, napkins, and four glasses
of cold milk. After we polished off a dozen brownies, which didn't
take long, we went up to my room. Hans sat at my corner desk and
worked on the map. C.J. used the computer station next to it, and
started entering sections of his report. Lizabeth spread her stuff all
over the rug in front of the closet, organizing papers for her report
and working on a Table of Contents. I couldn't help but notice she
had an awful lot of pages. I lay on my stomach on my bed,
skimming through a book, and taking more notes.

For the next hour, we worked pretty much in silence.

"Tada! I've got everything entered, " C.J. said, jumping up as he finished copying his new additions onto a thumb drive that he'd brought with him. "After Mrs. Jackson reads it over tomorrow, I'm going to be ready to print it all out. You know, it wasn't half as bad as I thought it would be."

"I'm in good shape, too," Lizabeth said. Of course, that was no surprise.

"I'll enter this new stuff I've just taken notes on, and Hans and I'll be ready to print out our report too," I said.

"The map is done," Hans announced, turning around. "Vat you think?"

He held up a gorgeous map. The lettering was straight and neat where he'd identified cities, lakes and mountains. He'd used colored pencils to brighten it up.

"It looks great," Lizabeth said, and I think I detected the slightest note of envy in her voice. Of course her report included a map, but it wasn't a hand-drawn one like Hans had made.

"It's going to be fun to share these reports next Wednesday night when everyone comes to school," she said.

"With cookies and cakes to sample," C.J. added.

I thought of our Tiroler cake that Mrs. Stahlein was bringing Wednesday night and couldn't help smiling. C.J. would take one bite and think he'd died and gone to heaven.

"Hey," Lizabeth said, changing the subject. "What's with Steve, anyway? He all but ruined Hans's map today, and it didn't really look to me like an accident. Yesterday, he ran you over, Jack. What's up with that guy?"

Here was my chance to come clean, to tell them what had been going on. Did I dare? My mind raced, but somehow I couldn't make myself say anything.

"Guess he's just a real klutz," I finally said.

"A *Dummkopf*," Hans muttered under his breath.

And the moment passed.

Thursday morning, I dropped my baseball mitt in the bottom of my backpack, well hidden under notebooks and library books. We all had World Series fever at school, and played ball whenever we could. I wanted to look good with my mitt. I went up to my bedroom to have some privacy while I hid my lunch money in my shoe. I felt silly even as I did it, but I thought it might be a safe place. When Steve and Cliff stopped me this morning, and found both empty pockets and no lunch bag, I'd tell them I was charging lunch.

I couldn't help but feel anxious as I approached the school grounds. My heart started beating faster. The lump under my sock where my money was hidden suddenly began to bother me, and I had to remind myself not to limp. If those guys suspected anything, I had no doubt they'd steal my shoes.

But to my surprise, Steve and Cliff weren't waiting for me. Maybe Steve was laying low because he'd been in trouble with both the librarian and the P.E. teacher yesterday, and he couldn't risk getting in more trouble today. Or maybe it added to his bizarre idea of fun to keep me guessing as to where and when he'd next pounce on me. I didn't know, but I was happy to make it safely into the classroom where I raised my hand to be counted for hot lunch.

The morning passed quickly enough with more division of fractions and fun independent reading, and then it was time for lunch. We had chicken nuggets with a dipping sauce, so it wasn't too bad. Best of all was the fact that in the cafeteria Steve and Cliff sat nowhere near us. I finally stopped looking over my shoulder and breathed a little more easily.

After we ate, C.J. said, "Come on. Let's get out there and claim a good piece of the playground where we can play ball."

I automatically looked around. Steve and Cliff were already gone. They often slipped out ahead of dismissal time. As everyone scrambled up from our table to go outside, I realized I'd forgotten to bring my mitt.

"Hey, I left my baseball mitt in the coat closet," I said. "Go ahead and stake out a good ball field. I'll meet you out there."

I ran back down the hall toward my classroom. As I went past the boy's bathroom, I saw Cliff just entering it, but no sign of Steve. I was relieved not to have to face them. I hurried straight to our room, pulled open the coat closet door, and stopped, puzzled. Where was my backpack? I had to look twice before I found it, and then had to convince myself it was really mine. It had been thrown on the floor, and the straps had all been unbuckled and tied in knots. It was definitely mine, with an identifying tag sewed onto the back. I picked it up and reached inside. My baseball glove was gone.

I felt like someone had punched me in the stomach, and for a minute I just stood there. Why had I ever brought my special mitt to school? Why had I thought that anything of mine would ever be safe again?

After only a month of school, our coat closet was a mess. It wasn't yet as bad as it would be come winter when we had boots and heavy coats, but it was bad. A few jackets hung on hooks while other sweaters had fallen on the floor to join empty paper bags and miscellaneous junk. I looked around, feeling desperate. Even though I knew my baseball mitt was gone, I kept hoping that somehow it had fallen out and was here somewhere amongst the trash. No such luck. It wasn't in my pack. It wasn't on the floor. It wasn't here.

For a minute I thought I might throw up. Steve! I hadn't seen him around the coat closet. In fact, he hadn't come near me all day, so I hadn't paid as much attention to him as I usually did. Letting my guard down again. But I knew, deep down, that Steve had taken my mitt. There was no way he could have known I'd brought it today, so he was probably fooling around, tying knots in the straps of my backpack and generally causing me grief, when he discovered it.

Losing my baseball glove would have been awful at any time. But now? Uncle Max would be flying out in a few days for the big World Series game. How could I face him and tell him that I'd lost the first baseman's glove he'd given me?

I gave the closet one more frantic search before I ran outside to join my buddies.

"What took you so long?" C.J. asked when I came running up.

"Someone took my baseball glove," I said.

"Are you sure?" Lizabeth asked.

"Yeah," I said. "I almost never bring it, but dumb me! I packed it today. When I just looked in the coat closet, I found that someone had been in there and tied all the straps of my backpack in knots. My mitt is gone."

We all looked at each other, and then Hans put into words what I knew each of us was thinking: "Steve."

"Let's go find that jerk and make him give it back," C.J. said. I couldn't help wishing that I'd had the courage to say that.

As C.J. spoke, he scanned the playground, looking to see where Steve was. We all spotted him at the same moment. Steve and Cliff and some of their buddies were playing back at the far corner of the field.

"There he is," C.J. said, pointing.

But before any of us could run in that direction, Lizabeth said. "Wait! We need help with this. We may think it was Steve, but we didn't actually see him take it. And he won't be dumb enough to have it on the playground with him. If we go running up there and accuse him, he'll just deny it. Then what?"

Yeah, I thought. Then what?

"I think we should wait until we go back inside," Lizabeth went on, "and tell Mrs. Hollis that your mitt has disappeared. Don't accuse anybody, and let her handle it."

I knew that this wasn't going over well with Hans and C.J. They clearly wanted to take Steve on, but they hesitated and looked at me.

"Your mitt, your call," C.J. said as I stood there, hesitating.

"Lizabeth's probably right." I hated myself even as I said it. Was I being smart, or a coward? "I'll tell Mrs. Hollis as soon as we go back in."

I could tell from the looks on their faces, that C.J. and Hans were disappointed, but they said no more. We spent a miserable time on the playground. We pretended everything was normal as we played ball, but none of us had our hearts in it.

The moment we all got back in the classroom, I managed to corner Mrs. Hollis and tell her about the missing mitt. Her face furrowed in concern. Lizabeth, C.J. and Hans stood with me. I was aware that, instead of sitting down, Steve was standing around, leaning our way as far as he could, trying to hear what was being said. I was sure he knew we were talking about the baseball mitt.

As soon as everyone was seated, Mrs. Hollis said to the class, "People, I need your help with something important. Jack brought his baseball glove to school this morning and left it in his backpack in the closet. It's disappeared."

Little whispers broke out among my classmates.

Before she had a chance to say anything more, I was astonished when, of all people, Steve loudly blurted out, "I think we've got a thief in our class."

I turned toward him, and I think my mouth was hanging open in surprise.

"This morning, before lunch," Steve said, "the strap on my wristwatch broke. I left my watch here on my desk when I went to lunch, and now it's gone."

"Are you sure you didn't put it inside your desk or in your pants pocket?" Mrs. Hollis asked.

"Yeah, I'm sure," Steve said. He pointed to his desk top as he said, "I know I left it right here. But I looked all around anyway. It's gone. And boy, is my dad going to be mad about this when he gets home from his trip this weekend. I borrowed it from him." Then he glared toward the table were C.J., Hans, Lizabeth and I sat, and continued. "My watch is gone all right, and I think I know who took it."

"Now wait a minute, Steve," Mrs. Hollis said. "Accusing someone of theft is very serious."

"I know," Steve said. "But when my watch band broke, that German kid, Hans, was back here sharpening his pencil. He heard my watch fall, and he picked it up and was looking at it. I saw him holding my watch with my own eyes."

Suddenly everyone in the class was staring at Hans. For a second Hans looked shocked, then he blushed red.

"*Nein,* no. I did not take vatch," Hans said, shaking his head.

"Did you pick up his watch, Hans?" Mrs. Hollis asked.

Hans said, "Yah. It fall on floor. I pick it up and I give it to Steve. I don't touch it or see it again."

"Did Hans give the watch back to you when he picked it up, Steve?"

"Yeah," Steve said. "And later he must have come back and taken it."

Mrs. Hollis said, "You have no reason to think that, Steve."

"Then where is it?" Steve demanded.

For what seemed to me like a very long minute, no one said anything at all, and then the room that had been filled with quiet murmurs began buzzing loudly like an angry beehive.

"I need everyone's attention," Mrs. Hollis said, and her voice cut through and stopped the murmur of voices. "This is very serious. We have a missing baseball mitt and a missing watch. But remember, at the moment, that's all we know. They are missing. We need to organize a search to find them."

Under her directions, a thorough search was made. Mrs. Hollis herself looked carefully through my desk, Steve's desk, and Hans's desk and the floor area near them. A team of kids went through the heap of stuff on the closet floor. Even though Steve and I both insisted that we hadn't taken either the watch or the baseball mitt out of the classroom, Mrs. Hollis nonetheless sent a couple of kids to check out the cafeteria and the school lost and found. Of course they reported back that neither item had been turned in.

Hans looked miserable. "I did not take vatch," he insisted, standing at our table. And although he wasn't asked to, he turned out both of his jeans pockets, showing them to be empty to anyone who would look.

"I know," Mrs. Hollis said. Gently she took both his hands. "Hans I know that you wouldn't do such a thing. It's lost somewhere, and we'll find it."

Although Mrs. Hollis sounded confident, and although the search was thorough, twenty minutes later we hadn't seen any sign of either the watch or my glove.

Cliff spoke up. "Maybe someone slipped in during the noon hour and took Steve's watch. I went to the boy's bathroom after eating lunch before I went to the playground, and guess who I saw running down the hall to our room? Jack."

Now all eyes were on me.

I felt myself turning red, just as Hans had done moments before.

"Yeah, I came to our classroom during lunch," I said. "To get my glove. That's when I found out someone had taken it. I didn't steal my own glove, and I didn't take Steve's watch, either."

As we searched everywhere a second time, I got myself excused to go to the boys' bathroom. Now that I'd been reminded of seeing Cliff slip in there when I was coming to the classroom to get my mitt, I thought maybe Steve had gone in there, too. He might have hidden my mitt there someplace. I dumped all the paper towels out of the waste basket, thinking my mitt might be at the bottom. But it wasn't. Discouraged, I went back to class to face the fact that there was no sign of either the wristwatch or the baseball mitt.

Mrs. Hollis said she'd make a complete report to the office, and everyone would be on the lookout, but there was little more that could be done.

The rest of the day was a total loss as far as I was concerned. My mitt was gone, and that's really all I could think about. I was sure that Steve had taken it somehow, although I had no idea where he might have hidden it. And I didn't know if he'd really lost his watch or if that was some sort of smoke screen he'd thought of to cover up stealing the baseball glove.

We were a sad bunch as we walked home from school this afternoon.

CHAPTER 10

Saturday morning about ten o'clock, I phoned C.J.

"Uncle Max called," I said. "Friday night will be my birthday party! He's flying into Denver that morning with six tickets for the World Series game. He'll rent a van to drive up to Boulder from the airport. It'll be big enough to take all six of us to the game that night."

"Great!" C.J. said. "We're going in style!"

Then there was a short awkward pause before C.J. asked, "Did you tell your uncle about losing your baseball mitt?"

"No," I said. The temporary excitement about my party and the World Series evaporated as I remembered my missing mitt. Actually, it was never far from my mind. It was sort of like the scab on my ankle. I'd forget all about it for a little bit. Then, absentmindedly, I'd scratch, and it would bleed again. "I should never have taken it to school. Man, I hate to tell him it's gone. I keep hoping that by some miracle it'll turn up before he gets here."

"Yeah," C.J. said. "It might."

We both chewed on that thought for a minute. It was a real long shot, but I held onto that thread of hope.

"Hey! I printed out my report on Italy this morning, and it's all ready to hand in Monday," C.J. said. There was no mistaking the pride in his voice.

"I printed our report out, too," I said. "Mom bought a fancy folder with plastic pages for me to put it in. Hans's map looks super. I was lucky to have him for a partner. It's the best report I've ever done."

"Now we're free!" C.J. crowed. *"Free!* Wanna go down to the park this afternoon and play some ball?"

Normally, that's exactly what I'd want to do. What better way to celebrate anything than playing ball? I hated the thought of going to the park without my mitt, but it wouldn't do any good sulking around the house all day and thinking about it.

"Sure," I said. "How about you come over here around one o'clock?" All of us lived within five blocks of each other, but my house was the closest to the park, so it made sense to gather here.

"I'll call Lizabeth to tell her about my party," I said, "and I'll invite her to come over here and go with us to the park."

"Okay," C.J. said. "How about if I bring one of my old gloves for you to use?"

When I didn't say anything, because I was still seething about my missing mitt, C.J. went on. "And I'll phone Hans. Maybe Geoff can come, too. See you at one."

That afternoon, Hans, C.J., Lizabeth, and I scuffed our way through leaves that had collected on the sidewalks as we made our way to the park. C. J. led the way, kicking a rock along in the gutter as we went, telling us he planned to get it all the way to the park. I wore C.J.'s old glove, and no one mentioned my stolen mitt on the walk down.

"My *Bruder* says he come down and join us pretty quick," Hans said. "Geoff vas on phone talking when I leave."

"Good," I said, and all of us smiled at the news. Geoff was certainly a plus on any ballfield.

Today was one of Boulder's great weather days, sunny with just the tiniest nip in the air. Summer was over, all right, but winter was still a long ways off. A few trees were already bare, but on many, the leaves were just turning, although a few of the maples were already bright red. I sniffed. It's hard to explain, but things smelled different in the Fall. I think it's the scent of baseball pennants!

When we got closer to the park, I could see that several guys were already playing in the grassy area over near the swings and slides. Uh-oh! My heart started racing. A few more steps sharpened my vision enough to confirm what I had suspected. It was Steve Mates, Cliff, and two other guys.

Lizabeth, ever the practical problem solver, must have spied them at the same moment, and said, "Let's head on over to the far side of the playground near the parking lot," and headed off in that direction.

C.J. and Hans quickly caught on to what was happening, and I noticed a red flush creep up Hans's neck and face. I knew he still felt hurt and angry that Steve had accused him of the theft of his watch.

"Yeah, let's stay away from them," C.J. said. "It's too nice a baseball day to let those creeps spoil it for us."

The big grassy field where we started playing wasn't far from the picnic area near the Rec Center building. There were three tables beneath trees and a couple of big trash barrels, up next to the edge of the parking lot. It wasn't long before we got into our usual routine of taking turns pitching, hitting, and fielding. There was plenty of distance to leave a good buffer between our outfield and the one that Steve and his friends were playing on. They ignored us, and we ignored them.

We'd been playing for about fifteen minutes when Hans hit a strong fly ball, and I went racing back for it. It was way over my head, no chance of catching it, and it rolled a long way. As luck would have it, Steve was in his outfield chasing a ball that had been hit toward me at the same time. As I scooped up our ball, I looked over at Steve, and what I saw made my heart skip a beat. Right there on his hand. He was wearing my mitt! I was sure of it.

Without really thinking what I was doing, I ran straight toward Steve.

"Hey, Mustard! What are you doin' here?" Steve asked.

By this time, I was up close to him, and could get a really good look. There was no doubt about it. Steve was wearing my baseball glove.

"Give me my mitt," I said.

"*Your* mitt?" Steve sneered. "I don't think so."

By this time, the kids from both ball games had figured out something was going on, and they came running toward Steve and me. C.J., Lizabeth, and Hans stood behind me, and Cliff and two of his friends stood behind Steve.

"What's goin' on?" Cliff asked.

"I want my mitt," I said, and almost surprised myself when the words jumped out of my mouth loud and clear. Usually I was so scared around Steve that I could hardly talk. Today, I wasn't scared. I was mad. This wasn't a brownie, or a bag of chips. This was my baseball glove, and I was taking it back.

"What are you talking about?" Cliff demanded, as he trotted right up to me, and stood almost nose to nose.

"That one," I said, not backing up an inch, and pointing to it. "The one on Steve's hand."

"This is my mitt," Steve said. "It's even got my name on it." He took it off and pointed to the black letters on the back of the glove that spelled out "MATES."

"No, it doesn't I said. "Look again! It says MAX , my uncle's name. He's the one who gave me the glove. You've just tried to change it from MAX to MATES, and anyone who isn't blind can see how you've written over the X with a 'T' and an 'E' and tried to squeeze in an S. That's my glove. Give it back."

"Try and get it," Steve said.

I dodged around Cliff and ran straight toward him. Steve quickly threw the glove in the air to Cliff, who started running toward the parking lot. I turned and chased after Cliff. Everyone else began running in that direction, too.

Whenever I got close to the glove, whoever had it threw it to one of the others. C.J. and Lizabeth were both too short to be of much help in this game of keep-away. It was always way over their heads. And Hans and I could never get quite close enough to intercept the mitt.

While this was going on, and we got closer and closer to the parking lot, I was suddenly aware of a lot of background noise. It was the sound of the local garbage truck pulling into the lot next to the trash containers. It maneuvered into place, and an automatic arm reached out from the truck, picked up one of the two big containers and shook it, upside down, over the back of the truck. I remember that as a little kid, I always liked to watch this. I thought these garbage pick-up machines looked like some sort of giant having a temper tantrum and shaking the trash containers.

There was a bang as one trash can was placed back down. Then the arms picked up the second one and the shaking process started again. The guy who sat next to the driver hopped out of the truck to pick up a box that had fallen over the edge of the truck bed. He pushed the two trash containers back into place and hopped back into his seat. Then there came the loud beep, beep, beeping of the garbage truck backing up.

At that second, Steve caught my mitt and was standing on the sidewalk. He seized the opportunity. He gave a giant heave, and I watched my baseball glove sail in a high arc and land right in the back of the garbage truck just as the driver pulled out of the lot and slowly started moving down the street.

With a hoot of laughter, Steve, Cliff and their buddies watched the truck drive off before they ran across the street and started walking up the hill toward home.

"Bye-bye, Mustard," I heard Steve yell as I stood there, stunned.

At this moment, Geoff drove into the parking lot in his old Chevy. He jumped out and came running up to us. "As he'd driven in, he'd seen my mitt sail through the air into the garbage truck. Hans quickly told him what had happened.

"After that truck," Geoff yelled.

One minute we were standing there, frozen in place like stick figures. The next, we'd all exploded into action. Each of us went running toward Geoff's car and piled in every which way. He started the car even as we were closing the doors and raced down the street in the direction of the retreating garbage truck.

Fortunately for us, garbage trucks don't move very fast and they stop often. We caught up with the truck at the second house past the park and Geoff quickly parked at the curb in front of the truck and we all ran back.

While everyone gathered around, I explained what had happened.

The sympathetic driver said, "Hang on, and we'll see what we can do."

The guy sitting next to the driver jumped out. "Now, don't any of you kids come climbing up here. You could get hurt, and we can't take that risk. But I'll take a look see back there. Maybe we'll get lucky."

While we stood by, the guy climbed into the bed of the garbage truck. I was holding my breath. This was crazy. I was sure he'd never find it. The guy was bent over that mountain of trash and was out of sight for a couple of minutes before he finally stood up, leaned over the top, a grin on his face, with my mitt held up high in his hand. "This it?" he asked.

The cheers that erupted let him know just how successful he'd been.

He tossed the mitt down to me and then climbed back down to the cab. The two of them drove off with a wave to acknowledge a chorus of thank-yous.

The five of us drove at a much less crazy pace back to the park. Sitting there in the back seat, I sniffed as I checked over the mitt. Maybe a slight smell of pepperoni pizza box? But it wasn't too bad off for its time in the garbage truck. What made my stomach churn were those ugly black letters spelling MATES written on the back. Maybe they'll come off, I hoped.

But most importantly, I'd stood up to that bully at last and demanded my glove back. How stupid or arrogant he was to think he could wear it around and that I wouldn't notice or do anything. Actually, in spite of the writing on the mitt, I felt good, as if a great weight had been lifted off me.

Back at the park, we played ball for almost two hours before we were all tired, and Geoff suggested sodas again.

While we sat around on the grass in the shade outside the Rec Center drinking our sodas, we filled in Geoff about the whole history of the stolen mitt. Of course the story about the missing wristwatch came out too, and it was clear that Geoff was angry about Hans having been accused of stealing it. Obviously Hans hadn't mentioned this at home in front of Geoff. He'd probably been too embarrassed.

"All the time Steve was making that big fuss about his father's stolen wristwatch," Lizabeth said, "he knew very well he had stolen your baseball glove."

"I wonder where he hid it?" C.J. asked. "We really searched that classroom and there was no sign of it."

"He probably stashed it somewhere outside," I said. "He had the whole noon hour recess out there on the playground to find a good place to hide it until he could safely pick it up."

"Yeah," Lizabeth agreed, "or one of his buddies from Mr. Senger's fifth grade class could have taken the glove inside and kept it for him until after school. We'll never know."

"I wonder if Steve's watch was even stolen at all?" C.J. said. "Maybe he made up the whole thing just to get us all in a big fuss about something other than the stolen baseball mitt. He might not have even worn his dad's watch to school at all."

"No," Hans said. "He had vatch. I see it fall. Band vas broken. I don't know vere it vent. Vat you tell Mrs. Hollis about the mitt?" he asked me.

"I don't know yet," I admitted.

"Well," C.J. said, "When you tell her about it, Steve is sure going to be in hot water."

"*Hot vater?*" asked Hans, with a puzzled look on his face.

"Big trouble," we all explained at once.

"Ah," Hans said. He smiled. "*Gut!*"

Geoff offered to give us a ride home before he left to hook up with his buddies, but we waved him off. We didn't have far to go, and he'd already given up a lot of his day to us.

As we all walked home from the park, I kept thinking about what I was going to tell Mrs. Hollis. I couldn't keep this a secret even if I wanted to. I had to tell her that I got the glove back or she'd keep asking everyone at school to look for it. And she'd definitely want to know how it turned up. But how would Steve react when she confronted him? Of course, he had plenty of time between now and then to think up a good story. But I didn't think even Steve could bluff or lie his way of this. He was caught.

An even bigger question hit me. How would Steve make me pay for telling our teacher on him?

CHAPTER 11

Hans and Lizabeth were talking pretty much as usual as we started walking back up the hill toward home. C.J. was out in front, kicking a rock again, planning to move it all the way to his house. I could never see what fun he got out of that, particularly kicking it uphill, but he always did it. I brought up the rear, fiddling with my baseball mitt, staring at the letters MATES now written on the back, and not paying much attention to any of them. I had a lot on my mind. It was kind of complicated, but it boiled down to deciding how much to tell who, and when to tell it.

I got jerked out of my thoughts though when a police car with sirens blaring made a sudden turn onto our street, zipped past us, and kept racing up the hill.

We all stared. This was no routine cruise of the neighborhood. That squad car was burning rubber. C.J. forgot about his rock and turned back toward us. "Wonder what's up?" he asked.

I expected to hear the siren disappear into the distance as it headed up into the hill. But instead, to my surprise, the squad car turned the corner and stopped just a couple of blocks up the street.

"Hey! Let's go see what's up," I yelled and started running. Hans ran right alongside me, and Lizabeth and C.J., with their short legs pumping, followed fast on our heels.

By the time it took us to run up the two blocks to the corner, several people had already gathered. Man, they got there fast! We were definitely not the only curious ones in the neighborhood. The crowd swelled as more people arrived from up and down the block. Everyone stood across the street from where the officers had parked. As I caught my breath, I realized with shock that the police car was in the driveway of Steve Mates' house. The onlookers were all quiet except for an occasional whisper, but there was plenty of noise coming from across the street.

A man in his early forties, wearing a gray sweatsuit, stood on the porch shouting and swearing while one of the officers tried to calm him down. He waved his arms wildly, staggered a few steps, and then caught himself on a porch rail just before falling. It was Steve's father. Steve's mother was out in the yard, too. I was pretty sure she was crying as she talked to the other police officer. Off by himself, slumped over with his face in his hands, sitting on the grass, was Steve. He was holding the side of his face.

When I finally managed to take everything in, I was really embarrassed. I didn't know where to look or what to do. I realized I was watching a family in trouble—big, private trouble. I felt that by standing there and staring, I was only making things worse. Feeling miserable, I glanced over at Lizabeth and thought I could see the same feelings reflected in her eyes. She, too, seemed to recognize we had no business being here.

"Let's get out of here," I whispered.

"Yeah," she said.

Wanting to slip away fast, I looked over at C.J. and Hans to motion them to leave with us, but they were standing there, gaping, open-mouthed, staring.

At this point, I saw one of the officers glance across the street at the growing crowd and then go talk to his partner. His partner walked over and said something to Steve, who got up and went to his mother. Both of them followed the policeman inside their house. Steve glanced back over his shoulder, but I was pretty sure he didn't see me because I was standing behind so many people.

The other police officer put an arm on Steve's dad's shoulder, but Mr. Mates violently shrugged it off. He glared across the street at all of us and yelled, "What are you staring at? Haven't you got something better to do with your miserable lives? Get out of here." His voice was kind of slurred, and I was pretty sure he was drunk. Then he, too disappeared inside the house with the officer following right behind him and urging him forward. Once inside, the policeman firmly closed the door.

As the door shut, it was as if the final credits had rolled in a movie theater. People sort of blinked, and the crowd immediately began to break up. There was nothing more to see, and maybe, like me, by this time they were finally feeling uncomfortable at what they'd witnessed.

A little group of observers near us gathered closer to Mrs. Engel, who stood five feet from me and was talking loudly to anyone who would listen. "Yes, I called the police. I was sitting out on my porch, having a cup of tea, when I heard yelling and screaming from their living room." She paused and shook her head. "Oh, I've heard it before, don't you know, but this was the worst ever. I expected it to quiet down pretty quick like it usually does. But this time it didn't."

"What happened?" someone asked.

"Mrs. Mates come running outside with Mr. Mates chasing right after her. He grabbed her by the arm, and slapped her, hard. I heard him say, 'When I'm not around, it's up to you to protect my stuff. You're too soft. You let this kid get away with everything. Now he's gone and lost my watch.'"

I didn't say anything out loud, but my mind was racing. Steve hadn't been putting on an act at school. He really *had* lost his father's watch. *And* he hadn't been exaggerating when he said how mad his dad would be when he found out.

"That poor woman puts up with a lot," someone muttered.

"She sure does," Mrs. Engle agreed. "When young Steve came running out the door, he was just in time to see Mr. Mates slap his wife again. Steve grabbed his dad's arm and tried to stop him. His dad let go of her arm just long enough to smack Steve. He send him flying. That's when I ran inside and dialed 911."

C.J. and Hans, who had been standing just in front of Lizabeth and me, whirled around to face us.

"The vatch!" Hans said loudly enough so that a couple people turned their heads. Hans lowered his voice before saying again, "You think they fight about the lost vatch?"

"Remember?" Lizabeth whispered. "When Steve told the class Friday about the broken band and the watch being stolen, he said he'd borrowed it, and he was worried about what his dad might do."

"He got that right," C.J. said.

"Let's get out of here," I whispered, and led the way.

We skirted the small cluster of people, and when we were a short distance off, Lizabeth said, "It must be awful to live in a family like that."

"Yeah," I agreed. I was thinking hard. Suddenly a lot about Steve was becoming clear to me.

We walked the rest of the way to my house in silence. I was feeling kind of sick at what we'd seen and heard, and I think the others felt the same way. Before we split up in from of my house to scatter in different directions, I said, "I want each of you to promise not to say anything to anyone about my mitt turning up with Steve in the park and how we got it back from the garbage truck. I want to talk to Mrs. Hollis about this myself, and I don't want anyone else to know. Okay?"

"Okay," they all said.

"Promise," I insisted.

They solemnly agreed. They were a sorry-looking group as they headed for their homes.

The moment I walked inside my house, Echo came running to greet me with tail wagging wildly. Standing inside the front door, I scratched Echo behind the ears which he loved. When he rolled over, I rubbed his tummy. I could hear the TV in the family room, and found Mom and Dad there watching some a news program.

"Hi," I said.

"Have a good game?" Dad asked, turning his head my way.

"Yeah."

"Did you see anything happening down the street?" Mom asked. "I thought I heard some sirens a little while ago."

"It was the police."

There must have been something strange about the way I spoke, because both Mom and Dad stopped watching the screen and turned to look at me.

Dad picked up the remote and clicked off the TV set.

"Why on earth were the police on our street?" Mom asked.

"Mrs. Engle called 911."

Mom looked alarmed. "Why?"

"She heard yelling, and then saw Mr. Mates hit Mrs. Mates and Steve," I said.

"Oh, how awful," Mom said. "Did they arrest him?"

"I don't know," I answered.

"Why don't you sit down, Jack," Dad said. "You're looking kind of pale. Are you okay? Do you want to talk?"

I sat down and for a moment I didn't say anything. The truth was, I'd been wanting to talk for days, but I hadn't known what to say. I'd felt like a coward, and I didn't want my parents to be ashamed of me. So I'd kept it all in. But now was my chance. It was time.

"Yeah," I said. "I think I'd better tell you what's been going on." Once I started, it all came pouring out, the stolen lunches and lunch money, the name calling that Steve used on me and my buddies, my bike tires that went flat by the end of Friday, and Steve flattening me on the first base line.

"Last Friday," I went on, "like a dummy, I took my baseball mitt to school. We're playing a lot now and I wanted to look good. It disappeared during lunch, and so did Steve's wristwatch that he said he'd borrowed from his dad. We searched everywhere but couldn't find the mitt or the watch. Down at the park this afternoon, we found my mitt."

I held my mitt up to them so they could see how Steve had used black marker to write his name over Uncle Max's name. Mom gasped and Dad got a hard set to his jaw as he stared at the glove. Then I told them how Steve had thrown it into the garbage truck and how we'd retrieved it.

"And from what Mrs. Engel said, I think Steve's dad got back in town and just discovered this afternoon that his watch was lost."

"This is terrible, "Mom said. "How long has all this been going on? Why didn't you talk to us about it before?"

"Steve jumped me a couple of times last May, "I admitted. "I figured he'd forget about it over the summer. Then it started up again. I didn't tell you earlier, because I thought I could deal with this myself. I didn't want to be a tattletale." I hesitated and then admitted, "Mostly, I didn't want you to know that I was a coward. I didn't know what to do."

Mom stood up and came over to the couch where I was sitting and gave me a hug.

"I probably wouldn't know what was best to do about it, either," Mom said, "but I'd never think you were a coward for avoiding a fight with two bullies."

"When you're faced with a problem," Dad said, "three heads are often better than one. Do your friends at school know what's been going on? Does he pick on them, too?"

"I didn't tell them what Steve does to me," I said, "but they're starting to get suspicious. Steve's always been a jerk, so we ignore a lot of what he says and does. But ever since last spring, I seem to be his main target. He calls my friends names and picks on them sometimes, but I think the only reason he does it is to get at me."

"Why does he pick on you?" Dad asked.

"I've been thinking a lot about that, but it only came clear to me this afternoon when I saw what Steve's dad had done to him and his mother. I think it may have started with the baseball teams this spring."

"The baseball teams?" Dad sounded surprised.

"How?" Mom wanted to know.

"You know how both of you come to my games, and Dad spends a lot of time and even helps coach the team. Steve's mom comes sometimes, but I've noticed Steve's dad is never there. When Dad plays catch with me in the yard or when Dad takes us to the Dairy Cream after a game to celebrate, whether we win or lose, I've seen Steve glaring at us. I think he's jealous."

Mom and Dad looked at each other and then back at me.

"I think he took my mitt because he knows how much baseball means to me. And that's where he made his big mistake," I said.

"What do you mean?" Mom asked.

"I mean that I'm finished being bullied by Steve. Even though I understand him better, I'm not going to be pushed around by him anymore. A brownie from my lunch is one thing. My baseball mitt is another. He'll find out Monday morning."

I think it was Mom's turn to look a little weird. "You mean you think you're going to school Monday morning and get in a fight with him over this?"

"I hope not," I said. "I'm going to try talking to him. I think that'll work. But yeah, if that doesn't work, we'll probably end up in a fight."

"Now just a minute," Mom said. "I won't have that. Doug!" Mom said, her voice rising as she turned to my dad. "Tell Jack he can't do that."

"Sally," my dad said, "I don't want our son in a fistfight, either. But Jack has thought this through. Let him tell us how he plans to handle this."

Mom looked at us as if she thought we were both crazy, but she let me explain.

"Monday is going to be real hard for Steve," I said. "I don't think he knows that C.J., Hans, Lizabeth and I were in the crowd when the police were there. But no matter what, word will get around fast about what happened with his dad. And I think things would be a lot worse for him if I spoke up to Mrs. Hollis during first period and told her in front of the whole class about what happened down at the park this afternoon. But I can't just be quiet about it. She has to know I've got it back, or she'll keep looking for my mitt."

"Of course you're right," Mom said. "Maybe I should call her tonight and tell her what's going on."

"Mom, I want to handle this," I said.

"How? What are you going to do?" Mom asked.

"I have a plan," I said. "I think it's a good one. So I'm asking you two to trust me and let me give it a try."

"Sally, we've got to let Jack try to settle this himself," Dad said. "We'll listen, Jack, but you've got to promise that whatever happens on Monday, you'll tell your Mom and me about it. You're not alone in this anymore."

As I told them my plan, I think I sounded pretty confident, at least I tried to, but my mind was in a whirl. Could I pull this off? Or was I really going to get clobbered?

CHAPTER 12

The inside of my head had never been busier. I could almost hear the wheels turning. It wasn't as if I were brilliantly hatching up one great idea after another. I just kept going over and over the ones I had. It was like some kind of perpetual motion machine in there with no time or room for thinking of anything else.

And all the time, I tried to look calm, putting on a good face for Mom and Dad. I knew if I panicked, they'd panic.

Every time I thought about Monday morning, I got flustered, but I wasn't really scared. It was funny, but I was over that. Part of being scared is not knowing what to do. I knew now what I was going to say and do, and I was ready. I think my poor brain just plain refused to go over the same old plan again and simply turned itself off.

Monday morning, Dad put his hand on my shoulder at the breakfast table before he left. "Good luck," he said. "We'll talk tonight." He looked sad, walking out the door and off to work leaving me to face whatever it was I had to deal with at school on my own.

Mom was worse. She packed me a lunch, as I'd asked, including three of my favorite peanut butter cookies, and she managed a wavering smile as I went out the door. But she looked scared. It wouldn't surprise me to find out she started crying as soon as the door shut. I think she thought I might come home in an ambulance.

I was glad I'd gone over to Hans's house Sunday afternoon taking the Switzerland report and leaving it with him to show his folks before bringing it to school Monday to Mrs. Hollis. I felt a lot easier in my mind knowing the report was safely in Hans's hands. It was one thing for me to risk my nose this morning if my plan with Steve didn't work out. It would be another thing to have Steve beat me up and destroy the Switzerland report which was Hans's work as much as mine.

No hiding lunch money in my shoe this morning, no different route to follow, no bike. No hiding. I walked straight to school. As I neared the back playground, I saw two familiar figures, Steve and Cliff, leaning against the fence. When they caught sight of me, they straightened up and started walking toward me. I didn't slow my pace or change direction. I hoped they couldn't hear how loud my heart was pounding. As usual, Steve planted himself in front of me while Cliff went to my back.

"Hey, Mustard! What's in the backpack today?" Cliff said. As he reached up to open my pack, he gave me a shove that almost knocked me off my feet.

I caught my balance and whirled around to face him, fists clenched. "My name is Jack," I said. "Remember that. And get lost. I need to talk to Steve—*alone.*"

Cliff couldn't have looked more surprised if I'd turned into a pickle-shaped green alien right in front of him or had punched him in the jaw without warning. And in fact, I was ready to do that next if needed. Cliff looked at me and then at Steve, uncertain of exactly what to do.

Turning to Steve, I said, "I was outside your place yesterday afternoon, and I saw what went down. Do you want Cliff to leave or stand here while I talk?"

Steve's eyes narrowed and I watched a flush move up his neck. Clearly he hadn't realized I was part of that crowd. Finally he growled, "Go on, Cliff. Beat it. I'll meet you at the door." Giving a malicious grin he added, "I'll save you a cupcake."

Cliff slouched off with a bewildered look on his face.

"Now, Mustard," Steve said. "What's in your lunch today, and what do you think a worm like you has to talk with me about?"

Steve reached up, grabbing me hard on the upper arm, and tried spinning me around so he could have easy access to my backpack. I dug my feet in and jerked free.

"Maybe you didn't hear," I said. "The name's Jack. And what's in *my* lunch is *my* business, not yours. You'd better remember that."

Steve gave me a hard poke to the shoulder.

I punched him right back as hard as I could, close-fisted, right in the chest.

I saw Steve's eyes widen, but he didn't say anything.

"And what we've got to talk about," I went on, "is that you're going to leave me and my buddies alone. From what I saw yesterday, I figure maybe you have a hard time at home. But I'm through being your free lunch, and I'm through being called names. So are my friends. It's over, as of right now."

"And what if I say it isn't?" Steve said. An evil smile spread across his face, and he made a small move toward me, but I stood my ground.

"You'd be making a big mistake," I said. "You'll get a fight, right here on the playground, and however it turns out, I guarantee all the teachers and yard supervisors will be involved."

Steve glared at me. I tightened my fists but held them at my side. I thought this might be it. But he didn't take a swing. He just stood there.

So I went on. "We also need to talk about *my* baseball mitt. You took it, but we got it back. You have two choices. I tell Mrs. Hollis what happened in front of the whole class this morning, or you and I go to her in private right now and you tell her exactly what happened."

Probably not more than a few seconds went by, but it seemed to me like a very long time before Steve spoke. "Keep your old lunch. Who needs it! But get this, *Jack*." Somehow he managed to spit out my name as if it were something dirty. "I'm not going to Mrs. Hollis and you're not telling her anything about that ratty old glove of yours."

"Wrong," I said. "We go find her and talk to her now, or I tell her in front of the whole class. Your choice."

Steve hesitated, and I watched him eye me up and down. There was no doubt that he was a lot bigger than me, but I think he knew how mad I was and that I was going do him some damage if we mixed it up.

"Let's go," he finally said, and began walking toward the front of the school. I walked along beside him without speaking or hesitating, stride for stride, although a part of me feared any second he'd step right in front of me and slug me.

As we passed the part of the yard where the little kids played, I was shocked out of my thoughts when a boy called out my name. "Hey, Jack. Watch this!"

It was the little guy I had helped with the big rings when he fell flat. I stopped and watched as he stepped off the climbing ladder, swung out on one ring, and caught another, before dropping and landing on his feet.

"See! I can do it now!" He was beaming with pride.

"Good for you," I yelled and without stopping gave him a big smile. I was hoping I could do it now too, face Steve down. With each step I took, I felt more confident.

We entered the front door of the school, and I led the way to the main office. I told the secretary that we needed to see Mrs. Hollis before school, and that it was important. The secretary, Mrs. Boland, knew every single person in the school by name. There was something in the look she gave Steve that let me know she'd already heard all about the police being at his house yesterday.

"Let me see if she's in the teachers' lounge or in her room," Mrs. Boland said.

She buzzed the classroom, using the intercom, and Mrs. Hollis answered, "Yes?"

"I have two boys here, Jack Tresidder and Steve Mates. They say they have something important to talk to you about before school. Is it all right to send them to your room?"

"Tell them to come right down," Mrs. Hollis said.

Steve and I didn't speak as we walked down the hall. I made sure not to hurry or slow my steps. I'd only get through this if I kept a tight grip on myself.

When we opened the door and stepped inside the classroom, Mrs. Hollis said, "What do you need to talk about, boys?"

"We want to talk about my baseball mitt," I said.

"Has it turned up?" she asked.

I looked at Steve and waited. I think he wanted me to do all the talking, but I wasn't going to.

"I took it," Steve finally said. "I came in the classroom during the noon hour last Friday, and I took the mitt. It was just a joke. When Jack saw me playing with it down at the park on Saturday, I gave it back to him."

"You mean when I caught you playing ball with it, you insisted it was yours, ran away with it and finally deliberately threw it into a garbage truck, so that I had to go chasing down the street after it," I said.

"Well, you got your stupid mitt back, didn't you?" Steve said. "That's more than I can say about my Dad's watch." He stopped glaring at me long enough to ask, "Did anyone find it, Mrs. Hollis?"

"No, and we'll talk about that in a minute, Steve," Mrs. Hollis said. "But right now, let's talk about the mitt. You stole Jack's mitt Friday and let all of us search for it while you knew exactly where it was, and then you went to the park Saturday, playing with the mitt, and when Steve saw it, instead of giving it back, you threw it into a garbage truck. Have I got that right?"

Steve remained sullenly silent.

"Right?" Mrs. Hollis repeated.

"Yeah," Steve said.

"Have you told Jack you were sorry for what you did?" Mrs. Hollis asked.

"Sorry," Steve muttered, staring at the floor.

"Jack, thank you for coming in with Steve this morning before school. You can go on outside now until the bell rings. Steve and I have some talking to do."

I got up and left. I guess I walked down the hall, but I may have floated. A huge load was off my back. I went outside and found C.J. and Lizabeth playing ball.

"Where's Hans?" I asked.

"He's already standing in line at the classroom door," Lizabeth said. "Holding on to your Melting Pot report."

Mrs. Hollis said nothing at all in class about my mitt or about the missing wristwatch. She looked happy at all the Melting Pot reports that everyone handed in. Steve kept his distance at recess and at noon, too, sitting at a table far from the one where Hans, Lizabeth, C.J. and I sat. Man! Did I enjoy those peanut butter cookies!

Every now and then in the cafeteria, I caught snatches of conversation. News of the police at Steve's house had spread. No one knew the whole story. One version said there'd been some sort of robbery. Another described a *big* family fight, with guns and knives. No matter what we heard, Hans, Lizabeth, C.J. and I didn't say anything.

That night at home, I told my folks everything that had happened, and they were pleased with the way I handled it, and satisfied that Steve had confessed to taking my mitt and apologized to me in front to Mrs. Hollis.

I told Mom about the rumors at school, and she said that she'd heard Mr. Mates had been arrested and taken to the police station. Social Services had been called in, and Steve's dad seemed to understand that if he hit either his wife or son again, he'd be locked up in jail for good.

"I don't know if it will have any effect on him or not," Mom said, "but I hope so."

"And if Steve Mates bothers you or your friends again, Jack," my dad said, "whatever else you do, you've got to promise to tell me about it."

"I will, Dad," I said, "but I'm hoping we're not going to have any more trouble from Steve."

On Wednesday morning, we had our regular classes at school, but in the afternoon we spent all our time getting everything in the room ready for our evening Melting Pot presentation. Mrs. Hollis had bought some pretty paper tablecloths with autumn leaves around the border and matching little plates and napkins. She had bags of plastic spoons and forks and lots of paper cups. Clearly she was expecting a lot of food to sample this evening.

We helped decorate two tables so there was plenty of room to set the foods from different countries. At another table, she put a big punch bowl ready and waiting for ice and punch to be added tonight.

About half an hour before the dismissal bell was to ring, Mrs. Hollis, said, "Okay, I think our room is looking good. We've rehearsed, and you all know what you're going to tell tonight about your country and which words you'll teach us all. Remember to point out the treat that you're bringing in to share which will be somewhere over on one of the tables. I hope lots of your parents and friends will be here to join us tonight. It's going to be fun!"

Hans and I exchanged happy smiles. Hans had said his parents and his brother were coming. Mom and dad had made arrangements to pick up Mrs. Stahlein and Mrs. Schwartz, and of course, the Tiroler cake.

"We have a couple more things thing to do," Mrs. Hollis said. "Clean out your desks and the coat closet. Each of you should clean your own work tables and desks first and then help straighten the room—the closet, the book shelves, whatever else you can. Be sure to get your coats and backpacks out of the closet and put them beneath your desks, so that I know everything is going home tonight."

Immediately, twenty-seven miniature cyclones hit our room. Papers, lunch bags, broken pencils without erasers, empty candy bar wrappers, all came out of their hidden-away places and were tossed into waste baskets. A couple times, kids had to take the baskets out and empty them into the big dumpsters at the side of the school and bring them back, only to have them filled to the brim again. Notebooks and books were stacked neatly.

People like Lizabeth, who always kept things neat, were quickly finished and helped with general straightening up. By five minutes to three, our room looked great.

"Way to go," Mrs. Hollis said, as she surveyed the classroom. Then she walked over to the coat closet. All the papers were off the floor, backpacks were gone, and only three jackets remained, hanging on hooks.

"These go home, too," Mrs. Hollis said. "Nothing gets left here this afternoon."

She walked over and picked up a light blue hoodie in one hand and a red sweater in the other. "Owners?" she asked.

Embarrassed, Michelle quickly scurried up to claim the sweater. Clearly, she'd forgotten it was there. It took his friends nudging him, until Malik recognized and reluctantly went up to take the blue hoodie.

"One last thing," Mrs. Hollis said. She held up a navy blue jacket. "Going once, going twice," she teased, bobbing the jacket up and down. Still no one came up to get it.

Mrs. Hollis looked in the neck of the jacket to see if maybe there was an identifying name printed on the label, but no such luck.

"Come on," she said. "It must belong to someone. I know you guys hate to carry home your jackets on a nice day like today, but it's cleanup day. Everything goes."

Finally she decided to check and see if there was a paper or something in one of the pockets that someone might recognize.

She pulled one pocket inside out, revealing a large hole in it. As she pushed the pocket back inside, a strange look came over her face. Then she reached down through the hole and into the lining and withdrew something silver. With a startled look on her face, she held it up. It was a silver wristwatch on a broken band.

"Steve," Mrs. Hollis said, "I believe this must be your jacket. You must have put your dad's watch in the pocket, and it fell right through the hole into the lining. You thought it was missing or stolen—but here it was, safe and sound, all the time."

Steve walked up to her and took the jacket. Then he took the watch and put it in his pants-pocket without saying a word.

I wondered how his dad would react when he got his watch back.

CHAPTER 13

On Melting Pot sharing night, Mom and Dad left our house early to drive us down the street to pick up Mrs. Stahlein and Mr. Schwartz. They were ready and waiting. Even though Mom had explained this was a very simple affair at school, Mr. Schwartz was dressed in a black suit with a vest and a snow-white shirt. He even wore those fancy things in his shirt cuffs, and it looked to me like they were made of real gold.

"Hello," Dad said, as he got out to open the car door for them.

I jumped out, too, and introduced Dad. Mrs. Stahlein handed me a cake to hold as they got in. I held it very carefully. I knew it must have meant an awful lot of work, but I was thrilled to see such a beautiful cake. It looked wonderful, and I knew it would taste even better.

"Wow!" I said. "Thanks a million. Boy, it looks good!"

As we started to drive away, I asked a question that had been on my mind. "You have a pretty yellow door on your house," I said. "That's unusual."

"In some old villages in Switzerland," Mrs. Stahlein explained, "houses have bright colored doors and little benches outside where people can sit and visit. Papa and I sit out there sometimes in the evenings."

Once we got to school and parked, we joined the stream of guests entering through the door as they dropped off cookies, finger foods, and cakes at the tables decorated with autumn leaves.

As promised, Mrs. Hollis had little cards ready, and I printed "Switzerland" on one and set it in front of the cake. This way people would know from which country each treat had come.

Parents and friends began seating themselves in folding chairs in a semi-circle at the front of the room facing our desks.

Hans and his family arrived just after we did.

"Hi, partner," Hans said, hurrying over to us. His parents, Mr. and Mrs. Ollig, and his brother Geoff, all sat with our group, introducing one another. Hans immediately started talking with Mr. Schwartz in German, and Mrs. Ollig and Mrs. Stahlein joined in. The rest of us talked baseball and the World Series. Hans and I finally left our families and guests to join C.J., Lizabeth, and my other classmates.

I felt more and more nervous as people kept arriving. They talked to one another, filling the extra chairs that were placed in back and along the sides of the room. I saw Steve come in with his mother and father, and I noticed that his dad was wearing a watch with a silver band on his wrist. I had wondered if they would come. The news about their family fight had died down a little, but it must still be hard to face people.

I found myself looking at Steve nervously, still wondering if he'd cause me trouble in any way. I tried to reassure myself by asking what Steve could do here in front of everyone. Unfortunately, I could think of more than a few things. He could manage to accidentally knock the Tiroler cake on the floor. He could make some sort of scene when Hans and I gave our report. He could spill punch all over my shirt.

My list of possibilities ended when, at promptly seven o'clock, Mrs. Hollis asked all of us kids to sit at our desks, facing most of the audience, and she greeted everyone. We all were to give a short report and teach our classmates and our guests a few words from the language of our country.

Hans and I took turns giving our report. I told a little about Switzerland. Hans showed his map and taught the class the three Swiss-German words. I pointed out the Tiroler cake giving credit to Mrs. Stahlein for baking it for us. Everyone applauded after each report, and Mr. Schwartz clapped especially long and loud for Hans and me.

Reports finished, we all milled about and tasted the wonderful foods. At one point, I found myself close to Steve. He glanced at me and I looked him in the eye.

"Hi," he said, and moved on as I returned his greeting.

I let out a little *whoosh* of relief.

Mrs. Stahlein had brought along a serving knife, and she cut tiny slices from the Tiroler cake. As I predicted, C.J. took one bite and rolled his eyes in joy. Mrs. Hollis had told us earlier to be polite and only take the smallest bite of anything to be sure to leave enough for our guests. But I know for a fact that C.J. wormed his way back into line and took another piece of the Tiroler cake. I had hoped that there might be leftovers, but no such luck. Every crumb was gone and all we brought home were an empty plate and a serving knife.

The rest of that week as I got close to school, I could feel my heart start to race. But Steve and Cliff no longer hung out waiting to pounce on me. Either I had gotten through to them, or all the meetings with Mrs. Hollis, the school counselor, parents, and social services had. Whatever the reason, the bullies left me and my friends alone. And I knew that if they ever tried to start up again, they'd have a fight on their hands. I was through being bullied.

The biggest and most lasting reminder of those two awful weeks was the black lettering on the back of my first baseman's mitt. Mom and I tried everything—detergents, scrubbing brush, and every spot remover known to man—but nothing would take MATES off the back of it. I still had my mitt, but it was ruined as far as I was concerned. I dreaded the moment I'd have to show it to Uncle Max.

One night during the week when Uncle Max phoned about the World Series to tell Mom and Dad where our seats for the big game were located and what time his flight got in, I asked to talk with him and took the phone. I told him that my mitt had been stolen and I got it back again, but that a kid had put his name on it in magic marker. I wanted to get that embarrassment over with before Uncle Max arrived and started asking questions.

"Hey, don't worry about it," Uncle Max said. "That old mitt must be pretty worn out by this time anyway. It's had a good life."

I put the mitt away after that and tried not to think about it.

Mom worked out all the details so that Uncle Max would be at our house early Friday afternoon. Hans and his family, C.J., and Lizabeth, were all invited to come over and have birthday cake. Then the Olligs would leave for the game in their car and we'd take the rented van down to the baseball field.

Mom said it would be too late to have a party afterwards, and we all needed a little something to keep us from starving until we could get to the ball park and eat the hot dogs she'd promised for our birthday dinner.

When I got home from school on Friday afternoon, a strange blue van was parked in front of the house. I broke into a run and rushed in the house.

"Uncle Max!" I yelled.

"Hi, there, buddy." Uncle Max came hurrying to the front door to give me a giant bear hug. "Happy Birthday!"

Soon mom sent me upstairs to get dressed. I pulled on my purple tee-shirt, a little worn from a lot of use, but I needed to wear my team colors tonight. I grabbed my Rockies baseball cap before running downstairs again. Echo was at my heels wherever I went. He knew that something was up.

By a quarter of four, all the guests had arrived. Geoff and Max immediately started exchanging stories about playing ball at Fairview. Dad and Mr. Ollig started talking baseball again, at first being very polite, but eventually arguing over who was the best pitcher or outfielder. Mom and Mrs. Ollig were already visiting together like old friends.

While all this yacking was going on, C.J., Lizabeth, Hans and I sat on the floor, talking and digging into what Mom called "substantial snacks," which she had placed on the coffee table. I pigged out on chips and avocado dip.

Anxious to keep us on schedule, Mom kept her eye on the clock and right at four-fifteen she announced, "Time for cake!"

She slipped out into the kitchen and Mrs. Ollig went to help her while the rest of us crowded around the dining table. When they came back in, the two of them poured tea, coffee and milk. Then Mom vanished into the kitchen. When she came back, she was carrying a masterpiece! It was a giant baseball-shaped cake, frosted in white with cherry-red stitching for decoration. On top were ten lighted candles.

We all *oohed* and *aahed*, then everyone sang Happy Birthday.

"Make a wish!" Mom said.

I did, and with a big breath, blew, wishing I was blowing bullies out of my life forever. Then I pulled the candles out of the frosting and dropped them in a little dish while Mom sliced the cake. Dad got busy, scooping a generous amount of chocolate or vanilla ice cream onto each plate before passing them around. Once everyone was served, we all dug in.

"I think there's just enough time for presents before we leave," Mom said. She handed me a box.

Some people carefully remove each piece of tape and ribbon and study the card before actually opening a present. Not me. I tore that package open in nothing flat.

"Wow! Mom, Dad, Thanks!"

I held up a Rockies jacket. It was just like the ones the team members wore in the dugout, black and silver.

"Can I wear it tonight?"

"Of course," Mom said.

"It's windproof and waterproof," Dad added. "You'll be ready for anything."

Lizabeth handed me a long tube, wrapped in silver with a purple bow at one end.

Everyone watched while I carefully pulled out a Rockies poster.

"Fantastic! Thanks, Lizabeth. This is going right up in my room."

"You're welcome," she said.

C.J. handed me an envelope. It held a funny birthday card and something else — a Rockies baseball card for my collection.

"Perfect," I said. "Thanks, C.J."

Hans handed me a box. "From Geoff *und* me," he said.

Inside was a white jersey with purple stripes. It said "Rockies" in front. When I turned it over, on the back it read "Jack Tresidder" with the number 20.

"Hey, thanks everybody. This is what I call a perfect birthday." I jumped up off the floor. "I'll be right back, but I'm going upstairs to change real quick. I'm definitely wearing this stuff to the Series tonight!"

"Whoa, buddy," Uncle Max said. "One more present to open." He handed me a package.

"But your present was the tickets to the game tonight," I said.

"This is just a little something extra," Uncle Max said.

I opened the box and could hardly believe my eyes. There was a brand new first baseman's mitt. I pulled it on, loving the smell of newness and the feel of the soft leather and I hit my fist into the pocket.

"Thanks, Uncle Max," I said.

"You're welcome! That old mitt was really worn out. I thought you needed a fresh start. Now run, and change," he said. "We can't be late tonight for the old ball game."

In record time, I peeled off my old purple shirt, pulled on the new white jersey and zipped up the team jacket. I lay the mitt right on my pillow. No way was I going to risk dropping it in the stands tonight.

Before going back down to join the others, I took a look at myself in the mirror on my bedroom door, in all of my great new Rockies stuff from my family and my friends. I grinned. My bullies were gone! Then I raced down those stairs to join my buddies on our way to a World Series baseball game.

ABOUT THE AUTHOR

P HYLLIS J. PERRY grew up in a small, northern California town. She attended the University of California in Berkeley. Then she began her teaching career. She taught school in California, New Jersey, and Colorado. In the schools where she taught, Perry found instances of bullying which is the underlying problem facing the characters in her book, *Buddies, Bullies, and Baseball*.

OTHER BOOKS BY PHYLLIS

Stand Up and Whistle

Bold Women in Colorado History

A Kids' Look at Colorado

It Happened in Rocky Mountain National Park

The First Rainbow

Colorado Vanguards

CONNECT WITH PHYLLIS

www.phyllisjperry.com

BOOK DISCOUNTS AND SPECIAL DEALS

Sign up for free to get discounts and special deals on our best-selling books at

www.TCKPublishing.com/bookdeals

Made in the USA
Middletown, DE
14 December 2019